Soulless Monk

Book II of the Inquisitor Series

Soulless Monk

Book II of the Inquisitor Series

Lincoln S. Farish

www.inquisitorseries.com

Praise for Junior Inquisitor

"Lincoln Farish is a gifted writer with a bold imagination and a talent for intrigue. You always want to know more with the turn of each page! Junior Inquisitor is a fast paced, roller coaster ride of Good vs. Evil, the timeless battle with monsters and other beings that shakes our foundations. Get your Glock ready, stay alert, and enjoy this devilishly clever trip through stacks of Pure Evil...not to mention bodies!!!"

Dr. Lynne Campbell, author of Jack Hammer

"Farish writes his tale with a deft hand and quick pace. The action starts early and is unrelenting until the climatic grand finale. Entertaining, educational, unpredictable, and a whole lot of fun. An excellent debut novel from an immensely talented author."

JD Goff, author of Hope 239

"Some jobs you'd describe as back-breaking. Brother Sebastian's is soul-clenchingly tough. The surprise of a story so outlandish is that you're with him all the way: feeling his pain and savoring his victories. And that's testament to the quality of the writing. Farish sets the scene and gives you all the back story necessary for you to buy into his hero's plight. But that's not all. Farish handles the action brilliantly and his use of gallows humour sits perfectly in context. Where this tale ultimately excels, though, is in its pacing and ability to put the frighteners on. When things get weird, Farish gets masterful. Neither overplayed, nor underdone, if your spine isn't tingling I'd get checked out by a doctor—you're probably half-dead or a borderline psycho!"

Geronimo Bosch, author of the Dominion City Blues series.

"A lot of urban fantasy these days seems to be dominated by kickass female protagonists with relationship issues. These are fine and dandy, but I prefer my reads to involve less romance and more action and horror. Junior Inquisitor fits that bill nicely for me. The action in Junior Inquisitor starts right away and doesn't let up often. The horror is quite horrific, and the enemies are definitely formidable. Sebastian's got his hands full. I also loved Farish's take on the supernatural: as befitting a novel about a warrior order of God, there were no shades of gray. The evil is EVIL. I'm glad they're rare, because the world would be in trouble if they weren't.
Final verdict: Junior Inquisitor is an excellent debut novel, a good quick read, and I will definitely be picking up the next one when it's released."

RL King, author of the Alistair Stone Chronicles

Dedication

For the women who put up with me—my wife and my girls. You make me a better man, a better dad, and a better writer

Acknowledgments

Danielle Fine for her patience, expertise, broad range of skills and information that helped me look almost masterful.

Bill Stiteler and the other beta readers who mocked until it was better.

Liza O'Connor and Rick Gualtieri, who still encourage me and pass on their wisdom.

Friends, like Stephen, and family, who put up with me muttering about my book, talking about my book, and generally being obsessed with my book.
Thanks for the booze and BBQ.

The many readers and fans who send my messages racing across the internet, RT my thoughts, jokes, and promo material, take the time to read my blog and always ask, "When is the next one coming?" My answer was "soon," but now it is "now."

Also by Lincoln S. Farish

The Inquisitor Series:
Junior Inquisitor

PRELUDE

Most of Thaddeus's body was in the subbasement. Once the ritual dismemberment was complete, the individual pieces had been placed into reliquaries sealed and warded to prevent the parts from re-aggregating. Occasionally, a box would shudder slightly as a piece banged from the inside, trying to escape.

An intricate and eye-watering design had been hurriedly dug into the dirt floor by desperate men not wanting to die. It, along with the other wards, was energized by human sacrifice to keep the location secret from those who would bring Thaddeus back. Runes, splashed onto the walls in human blood, twisted and squirmed, waiting to be activated or to destroy the mind of anyone who stared too long. The decades of energy and blood that had been spilled here made the room almost alive. Aware. It smelled of fear and pain. It whispered malevolent madness. The dismemberment was merely the latest depravity, nearly not worth noting.

The house above the room—constructed for a man of peculiar avarice, long since dead—was now a leftover relic, never rebuilt, slowly collapsing into itself, like a rotten tooth of the insane. The local teens didn't use it, nor did druggies. Even animals, always looking for a place to hide or rest, avoided it. Lurking in plain sight, the house sat, waiting.

The door to the subbasement was forced open, groaning in displeasure or warning. A stream of light pierced the gloom, only to be blotted out by a man so big he almost couldn't fit through the doorframe. With jerky, puppet-like movements, he stomped down the wide steps, his vacant expression never wavering, except when he blinked in a slow, reptilian fashion.

"Stop!" a squeaky voice demanded, freezing the enormous man in place a few steps short of the dirt floor.

An average-sized man, small in comparison to the first, appeared at the top of the steps and made his way down. He held aloft a glowing, snapping ball of fire attached to a chain. Flaming drops fell from the ball but never reached the floor.

The new arrival's head was only partially covered with light brown hair, but he compensated with a magnificent set of sideburns—the type not seen since the Civil War or without a mullet at the local go-kart track. The sideburns were brushed and oiled daily and gleamed in the light. This magnificence was tempered by the rest of his physiognomy. His front teeth protruded, his eyes bulged, and his skin was dry and chapped. Still, he descended proudly, head held high and a swagger in his step, fully expecting the world to be in awe of his magisterial facial hair and power.

After shoving and squeezing past, he stopped at the last step above the dirt floor. Holding his light high, he examined the room. There was a cruel glint of dark wisdom in otherwise soft blue eyes as he peered around, searching for clues and traps.

"Yes," he muttered after a moment, "I've found him." He turned his head toward the large man, who remained motionless beyond slow, automatic blinks. "Go. Bring the sacrifices. The dreamer has been away too long."

CHAPTER 1

James

I felt more than heard the demonic scream, the cry of innocence being sacrificed on a blood-soaked altar.

Bright red blood gushed from my nose, spilling onto the table and my breakfast as I staggered up from the kitchen chair. More veins and arteries ruptured, filling my mouth with coppery-tasting slobber, followed by the digging, like a rusty knife burrowing through my brain. I clasped my hands to my head in a vain attempt to stop the damage. For a moment, the world took on a reddish haze as one of my eyes filled with blood. The scream was the rebirthing wail of my former master, the damage just a taste of what was to come. Two years had passed, and as promised, Thaddeus had returned.

As I sat down heavily, reality set in. If I didn't act soon, I was dead. All my ambitions would be scattered like sand before the wind, and I could not let that happen. Even though I'd prepared, and prepared well, it wasn't enough. The manacles should've worked. Bound by the silver and meteoric iron, any of the magi would've been powerless, unable to use magic, and doomed to a quick death. Anyone but Thaddeus.

"Betrayal!" Thaddeus had screamed when I'd slapped the manacles on him with gloved hands. Though his skin blistered—welts forming and popping open to weep a dark fluid that was not blood—the manacles slowed him but couldn't shut him down completely. With a few words and a wave of my hand, I'd magically torn his imp from his chest and sent it back to Hell. Despite his chest being open to the air, skin peeled back and broken ribs jutting out, he'd swung and launched me across the room. A setback, but I'd prepared. Those still loyal were eliminated by the rest of my group, and then the knives came out.

Thaddeus had taunted us through cracked and bloody teeth. "You will all die for this." He was naked, bleeding from a dozen wounds, manacles restricting his movements, but still deadly. He swiveled his head until his gaze fixed on me in the back. "Your suffering will be spoken of in whispers in the darkest corners of Hell!" he screamed and then laughed in a wet, chittering way.

He'd already killed three of us, and blinded Sammy, and he still refused to die. Parts sliced off by silver-plated daggers wriggled back to him, to be reabsorbed into his body. He should've been unnerved by my treachery, begging for mercy. He was defeated, facing his end, and yet he knew it wasn't true, he knew he would return, cheating death. The blades rose once more, and Thaddeus let out another cry as the silver cut and burned him. One arm hung from the manacles, severed at the shoulder. Despite this, he shuffled forward a step, and Bill didn't back away fast enough. Thaddeus lifted Bill one-armed off the ground and crushed his neck, the wet snaps rocketing around the room like muffled gunshots. I dashed forward, and snatched the arm free through the cuff of the restraints, pulverizing the wrist and hand bones as I yanked it through the too-small opening. I skipped back before he could turn on me and placed the arm into a reliquary, snapping the lid shut. The silver inlay and sigils carved into the box magically isolated the arm from Thaddeus, weakening him.

He must've felt the loss, as he sagged to one knee and dropped the body. The knives gleamed weakly in the light as they hacked and chopped again and again. When it was safe, Thaddeus reduced to fleshy ribbons, I resumed hands-on command, and the ritual dismemberment began. The body still tried to re-form, but it was too late. Thaddeus spat defiance until the end, when I removed his head. He'd warned us, between killing the lesser ones and laughing at our mutiny, that Hell was a pit stop for him, not a prison. I should've believed him.

That scream meant he'd done it. I needed to fight him, now, before he could get back to full power and collect new minions. If that happened, no distance was too great, no protection sufficient. He would find me, and fulfill his promise. My time of reckoning had come, if I let it. I'd fled my first family, betrayed my second, and was about to abandon my third. Peter had it easy. All he did was deny Christ three times.

I've had many names over the years. My parents, in a literary fit, named me Othello, which meant I spent my school days learning to fight or run away from bullies. Other than that, I had a typical childhood, for the most part. I had the usual number of friends and was involved in normal boyhood pursuits. Things were fine, until puberty hit, and I began to see the evil ones. Worried about drugs, my parents had me tested. When I came back clean, they thought I might be like my Uncle Owen, who'd ended up living on the streets, collecting bottles and howling at people. They tried doctors and drugs, which made me sleepy and happy, but didn't change what I saw. Didn't change the way the evil ones looked at me. I knew they were coming to get me, sooner or later. Finally, my parents had me committed, "for my own good."

The hospital was a slaughter pen, with me the dumb animal awaiting death. I ran away, never looking back, afraid of what I'd see, convinced I was being pursued. For the next several months, I was homeless, never staying in one place very long, dreading the day one of the evil ones found me. I learned how to scam and steal. How to survive on food that would've made others hurl. Where I could sleep safely. Not to trust anyone. To use them for as long as I could. That life came to an end when I got sick. I'd managed to con a dorky kid named Chip Nettles into letting me stay with him for a few days, but halfway through the first night, I was feverish and vomiting.

"Chip," I cried, sweaty and shivering, "don't let them get me. You gotta hide me. They're coming." Already in trouble with his parents for letting me stay in their basement, Chip borrowed their car and dumped me in front of a shelter. I staggered in, screaming about betrayal and the evil ones, before collapsing.

It turned out to be a lucky break for both of us, which is why I've never hunted Chip down. He'd driven me to the All Saints Homeless Shelter run by the Benedictines. When I awoke, I was at a monastery, and safe. Brother Gerald was sitting in a chair next to me when I finally was lucid. He gave me water and a little food.

"You were in a bad way when you came into the shelter," he said in response to my questions. "We drove you out here so you'd be safe while you recuperate."

I was wary—I'd heard what happened in such places—but Brother Gerald was a master of manipulation. In three days, I trusted him and wanted to stay, at least for a while. Once he'd hooked me, he explained why I was the way I was.

"Othello, you have a gift and a curse," he said in a soft voice, his rough features furrowed. "You can see witches."

I laughed at him, but he didn't get upset. Instead, he introduced me to others who could see what I saw. Had it been one or two, I would've scoffed at such nonsense, but I met a dozen. Some were old men, others just out of high school. Each told me about seeing their first witch and what had happened. I was still sure it was some conspiracy or joke, and said as much…until they showed me the cat.

Brother Gerald led me to a small, empty classroom.

I looked around nervously. "Why are we here?"

"You have doubts," he responded.

I fidgeted in my seat. I felt safe for the first time in years, but what Brother Gerald wanted me to believe was too much. Too crazy.

Another monk wheeled in a cage. Inside was a cat, larger than any I'd seen before. It was screeching and jumping around. Long toes the size of fingers, with a good two inches of claw on them, reached through the bars, trying to hurt something.

I tried to be cool and unimpressed, crossing my arms and leaning back in the chair.

"Go ahead Othello," said Brother Gerald, gesturing at the enraged animal. "Get a good look, and you'll believe."

Acting nonchalant, I sauntered up to the cage.

It's just a big mutant cat.

Then it spoke.

"Yes, come here and let me taste you," it said in a hissing voice.

I could see its mouth moving. It was talking. To me. I fell backward, and it laughed in a screechy sort of way. I scrambled away on my hands and feet, keeping my eyes on it and clenching my bladder.

"Let me out of here, you shit-eating, faithless worm, and my mistress will kill you last," it said.

After a few more curses and warnings, the monk in charge of the cat wheeled it back out. I never questioned Brother Gerald again.

The monks gave me a more commonplace name, James, and told me I would have to stay in the shadows from then on. They taught me how to survive in a world of evil. I fought witches, I slew monsters, I went to mass regularly, and I was content, for a while. Then Brother Gerald died, and it hit me: I would join him soon. My life was finite, and I wanted more. I deserved more.

I didn't lose my faith; I realized the feebleness of it. If faith couldn't keep

Brother Gerald alive, how would it protect me?

Faith can't win against supernatural creatures and demonic influences, I thought, flipping through a grimoire I'd neglected to turn in.

It spoke madness to me, but I knew my will would prevail. I could learn and not be corrupted. I would be the master of magic, not its slave.

My faith was a tiny flickering candle trying to illuminate a football field on a foggy night.

It's not enough.

I wanted to live, and needed more power than simple faith.

Going even further, I left my old life. Eventually, I became Thaddeus's student, his slave, and he showed me the limitlessness of power coupled with will.

"The exercise of power is only constrained by those with even more," he told me once after we'd brought a rogue witch to heel.

I looked down at her as she bled out on the carpet—her minions slain, her life forfeit—and agreed. Thaddeus didn't talk, he demonstrated. He showed me the truth through action.

"There are no laws, natural or otherwise. There are only the powerful and the weak," he told me.

A while later, I did a scrying—reading the future in the entrails of a sacrifice. I shoved the ensorcelled emerald down his pudgy throat and cut him open with a crystal knife. Eating the ropey gray intestines of the coney, I began to see. I saw my true self and what I could be. I saw all possibilities, all the knowledge that would be available to me, if I stretched out my arms and mind. I was too small for that destiny, unready, afraid to take with red claw and fang the power that could be mine. The vision changed, and I saw myself pleading for my life and then...nothing.

"What did you see, slave?" asked Thaddeus.

I lied. "I saw myself grow strong, powerful. Walking through the first gate with a crown of fire."

His eyes glowed and his face darkened. "I think you saw yourself begging for mercy," said Thaddeus. "Groveling on the ground, weak and helpless before your betters. We shall see what occurs."

I began to forge Thaddeus's manacles the next day. For weeks, I toiled in secret, working with the silver and meteoric iron necessary to contain his terrible power, creating them link by link, curses and sigils of power engraved into each one. I bided my time, professing subservience until the moment I led the revolt against him. All who survived were sacrificed to keep Thaddeus's location secret, and I fled again.

I didn't go far, just across the border to Taos, New Mexico. I needed to stay close to the crypt. Part of me had known this day would come. Thaddeus would not be held in Hell for very long—there was too much evil he could wreak on earth, too many ways he could make a deal to return.

CHAPTER 2

Taos is an eclectic community of leftover hippies, those not quite good enough for the Aspen or Telluride crowd, the occasional Hollywood cowboy, and simple, blue-collar folk. Mindless cattle. I had decided on Taos as it was small enough to avoid my former brothers, who must've known about my change of heart, and big enough to remain anonymous. Assuming I could control my impulse to burn the place down and send those fools to Hell.

Even though I'd betrayed him, Thaddeus had taught me much. Right and wrong are just concepts foisted on us by the weak, abstracts that have little value in my life. Those foolish theories had been cast aside; survival and freedom are what matter in life. From the Brethren, I learned how to fit in. How to become part of almost any group, even when all I want to do is sacrifice them. Feel hot blood wash over my face as the light dims in their eyes and they take that last shuddering breath. Instead, I smile pleasantly, and wait.

In Taos, I took a new name, Rik O'Banion. I knew the alias would hold. The real Rik had been a runaway who'd died from bad cocaine in Portland, Oregon back when I was with the Brethren. Thanks to me, the body was never found. I swiped his ID and took the body to a house boat I borrowed. A one-day "fishing" trip, and the body was miles beneath the ocean. A deep background check would show I hadn't paid taxes or had a permanent address in a while, but the driver's license was good, and I could explain the rest with youthful wandering. I hadn't used the ID before arriving in Taos, so the Brethren didn't know of it. Maybe even back then I'd known I was a Judas.

I got myself hired on as a bartender at a cop bar, and set about seducing a wife in order to secure my future. There were many advantages to picking a cop. As a part of the cop family, I got the three things I needed: some protection, intel, and the benefit of the doubt. The seduction was pathetically easy—Olivia was over thirty, had a child, and not many prospects. She was olive-skinned, courtesy of a Hispanic mother, had full, sensuous lips, dark medium-length hair, and eyes so brown they were almost black. When she was younger, in a fit of teenage rebellion, she'd gotten a tattoo of a Hopi kachina, the pipe player, on her left foot. She might've been pretty. I didn't care.

None of it mattered. She was discontented, and that, I could use. Her neediness radiated like a searchlight in the dark. Doubt and worry visibly dogged her every step—was she a good enough cop, could she handle being "one of the guys" but still be a woman, was she a good mother despite all the time she had to spend away from her son? It was tiresome and had driven off many men before me, leaving her feeling guilty over a string of failed relationships. It took me a few seconds to see this and another few to figure out how to use her weaknesses to control her.

When we were introduced, I went with flattery. "Cool. So how many people do you think you've saved?"

The usual question a cop gets—"how many people have you killed?"—puts the person on the defensive, not-so-subtly implying that they're a murderer who hasn't yet been brought to justice. Stupid, but the mindset of cattle. Olivia, like most cops, was proud of the work she did, the people she helped, even the ungrateful ones who should've been culled. She actually blushed and stammered for a minute. Vanity is the easiest emotion to manipulate.

Most of the time guys dominate a conversation, and women resent it, a little. They want to be heard. It doesn't matter what the topic is, they want to be able to voice their opinion as well. They want to tell their stories. Being quiet made me appear sensitive and understanding, when what I was really doing was gathering facts to use later. Of course, as a cop, she asked me questions as well. I kept the answers simple and didn't elaborate.

She picked up on this, quirked one eyebrow and looked searchingly and suspiciously with those large brown eyes. "Why are you so quiet?"

It was more than a question, it was a challenge, but I was way ahead of her. "I want to hear about you. I can brag about myself anytime."

She melted. She was mine; it was just a matter of time.

Cops are pack animals, men and women looking for a simple code to live by in their attempt to understand the world. The power to compel others appeals to their sense of right and wrong. They also tend to place people into categories: one of us, to be protected, and potential criminals. Obviously, I couldn't let myself be placed in the criminal category, but being tagged as someone to protect would've fucked me over too. A cop will protect you if needed, while silently cringing at your weakness. I needed to be in the respected category if I ever wanted to be treated as a near-equal and not sneered at and mocked. No woman can love a man but not respect him, nor will a woman put up with her man being derided. To pull off my seduction, I would need the respect of her co-workers, but in such a way that it didn't challenge their authority.

I decided on beating someone up, mostly for giggles. Sadly, I had to restrain myself. I couldn't come across as a veteran of unarmed combat—that would raise questions, and cops are a curious bunch. So I had to be able to handle myself physically, but just barely. I had to lie, again. It was easy. Fun.

I was closing the bar one night, and a drunk, one of the reserve cops, who had few friends and a penchant for over-physicality, decided he didn't want to go home. He'd been in several times before, blustering, but never any real trouble. He was a large, beefy man—the kind who'd played linebacker in high school, and then, when faced with real life and the loss of cheering crowds, became bitter and sought salvation in alcohol. His athleticism morphed into slovenliness: fat replacing muscle. He was in a slow spiral down to cirrhotic death, driving away friends and then loved ones, until finally he was alone and could gnaw on his bitterness in solitude. I'd enjoyed his self-hatred, reveled in his self-destructive tendencies, and slid him a few extra beers to put him over the edge. Now it was time to act.

The other cops waited to see what I would do. Could I man up and solve the problem or did I need their help? Essentially, was I worth their respect?

The four other late night drinkers—the vice squad for Taos—turned slightly in their chairs and watched.

Without looking directly at my audience, I walked over to where the drunk hogged a four-top table littered with empties, radiating hostility. I came up on his side to make it more difficult for the cops to see exactly what I was doing and to force him to turn, which would irritate him further.

"Come on, buddy. I got to lock up," I said.

"Get fucked. I'm still drinking."

"Really, you gotta go." I pointedly did not look back at the vice squad. To do so would be to admit weakness, that I needed their help, that I couldn't handle myself.

He eyed me through a drunken haze, his blue eyes watery and bloodshot. Liquid courage, and the fact he outweighed me by a good seventy-five pounds, made him dismiss my request. He snorted in my direction. "I'll be done in a few minutes. Go mop a toilet."

I didn't want to bother with verbal back and forth for ten minutes until he finally decided to be angry. With a slight grin, I poked him in the shoulder, a move sure to infuriate him. "No. You gotta go."

He roused himself from his chair and took a swing at me. It was slow, easy to avoid. He was strong, but unskilled past the wade-in-and-punch-'til-they-drop level. I trapped the hand, turned it over to lock the wrist, elbow, and shoulder in a line then took a short step back. Turning in a tight circle, I kept my elbows in. It was a simple, easy, relatively painless counter to a punch—one of the first I'd learned at the monastery. And while it didn't hurt much, there wasn't a lot the drunk could do but go where directed. I spun him down onto the floor in a slow, controlled fall. Once he was face down, I placed one foot on his shoulder blade to keep him from wriggling. Normally, I would've slammed him to the floor and stomped on the arm, breaking the humerus and tearing it out of the socket. Under the eyes of the Taos police force, I went with moderation.

"Okay, okay, get off me. I'll go," he said.

The lie made me grin again. The moment he got up, he'd take another swing. Alcohol really reduces the self-preservation instinct, and he wasn't in enough pain to drive the stupidity from his brain. I dropped the arm and slid back a bit toward a column. As predicted, he got up, whirled toward me, and charged. I stepped aside and turned then gave him a bit of a push into the column as he went by. Drunks are like Superballs: the harder you drop them, the more they bounce. After his face-plant, he rebounded with his back toward me. I swept one of his legs up, and grabbed the collar of his sweat-stained shirt, pulling him back and toward the floor. Unprepared, and clumsy from the alcohol, he fell flat on his back, stunned for just a moment.

I put one foot on his neck, slowly looked down at him, and said, "I really need to lock up."

He blinked up at me stupidly, the realization that he was in danger only now seeping into his beer-soaked brain.

The cops had seen enough. They got up and strolled over to me, circling the two of us.

"There a problem here, Rik?" someone asked. A quick glance showed me it was Sergeant Pullman. His voice was flat, without inflection; he was in professional law enforcement mode.

"No," I said. "It's just closing time".

"We've got it from here," he said. An order, not a request.

I stepped off the drunk's neck and far enough away to avoid any last-minute swings, and let them handle the problem. The two nameless officers each grabbed an arm and helped him to his feet. He was still wobbly and didn't resist as they cuffed his hands behind his back.

"Let's go, Glick," said one, while the other read off his Miranda rights, and they led him out of the bar.

Sergeant Pullman turned and faced me. His expression was neutral, but his brown eyes were lit up with questions. He was going to try to find out if I was lucky or a threat. Lieutenant Wolf, whose face matched his name, sidled to my other side, watching my reactions as Pullman questioned me.

"I don't want him back here," I said, giving a fake shiver as though coming off an adrenaline rush. "It could get bad. He might hurt someone."

Pullman's smile was as false as my shiver. "Don't worry, he won't be back. I don't think he'll have his volunteer badge any longer."

Lieutenant Wolf nodded in agreement.

"So," said Pullman slowly. "How did you learn to handle yourself like that?"

I had to convincingly downplay my experience, or there would be more questions and suspicion. "I took Hapkido years ago, taught little kids to help pay for school. Still practice a bit, mostly just to keep limber for running."

He frowned and, to assert his dominance, said, "Next time, let us handle the drunks."

"Of course, Officer," I replied, showing that I wasn't trying to be the alpha dog.

Satisfied that I wasn't a danger to the public or, worse, a threat to his authority, he smiled again. "How are things with you and Olivia?"

I shrugged. "It's only been two dates so far."

"You hurt her, and we'll come down on you like a ton of bricks." Now he wanted to make sure I knew my place. I was not one of them.

I smiled back at him, trying for a rueful expression. "Sergeant, if I hurt her, you'll find me just outside town, staked out over an anthill."

They both laughed, and I kept my smile up. Just another innocent member of the community.

CHAPTER 3

It took Olivia three dates to determine I was husband material, and a few months later, I was. I pretended to be a dutiful husband—helping with her ignorant lump of a son, maintaining the house, and keeping up my skills and physical fitness as best as I could. Magic would show up like a beacon through the ether, calling attention to myself, but I could practice other skills, like the occasional house breaking, or an anatomy lesson on a derelict who wouldn't be missed. I allowed Olivia to believe she'd taught me how to shoot, so I could get access to the police range. I always made sure I had a few stray shots, like any amateur would. No one ever recognized the occasional pattern in the paper; to them, it looked like I'd jerked the trigger, or over-thought the shot. Common mistakes.

My plans worked well. As the husband of a cop, I fell into a small gray area, like a District Attorney: not a cop, but one of the family. And, as a bartender who could slide them the occasional free drink while asking for nothing in return, I was a favored member. I had the cops keep watch for me. A simple explanation, that I'd run afoul of a gang a few years ago, meant they kept an eye out for anyone strange coming into the area. Nothing in writing, nothing official, just friends helping each other out. Everything was going fine, until this morning.

Recovering from the scream, I wrote a quick note that I was going camping—one more lie in a sea of lies, but one that would buy me the time I needed before anyone came looking. I doubted I'd ever need my cellphone again, so I left it and grabbed my "at home" gear—things that didn't look like weapons to anyone but a magi—and some rope and pulleys.

I drove north on highway 64 then turned east toward the mountains. At the end of Pueblo Canyon Road, I parked the car and hiked south toward the Kit Carson Forest. The sun filtered through the trees, making grotesque shadows. It was excessively quiet with few animals about. It made me wary and slowed me down as I skulked through the woods, checking to make sure I was alone and not headed into a pot field or ambush. Dopers weren't really a concern, but I didn't want to have to leave bodies behind just yet.

Normally, it was a quick climb up a ridge and then halfway down the other side, but this time, it took me almost ninety minutes to spot the rocks covering my cache. Even then, I waited for several minutes to see if anyone would reveal themselves. Finally, convinced nothing was out of place, I approached the rocks. When I'd stashed my gear, I'd driven a piton into the underside of one of the boulders. They seemed immovable, but with a rope and pulley system, they could be levered up. I'd padded a tree branch when I set the cache up so the rope wouldn't scar the tree and possibly draw curious eyes, but this time, I didn't bother. A cache was good for one visit, after which it was burned, unusable—a lesson hammered into us when I was training with the Brethren.

Once everything was rigged, the rock tilted up as if it were hinged, revealing my black Pelican cases. I pulled out all the gear I thought I might need. My 9mm Glock was a replacement for the one the Brethren had issued me. It was a generic model, not customized to my grip or engraved, but it would do as a backup weapon. The next things out were my MP-5 with silencer, and a Mamba sling that attached to my battle vest and kept my hands free when I didn't need my weapon. When I was suited up, the barrel hung level with my knee like a wilted black feather. I pulled out the magicked human hand holding my spells. On one finger was an over-sized ring, set with a large porphyrite stone, a mineral prized by magical folk. A dark, rich royal purple, it was able to store vast amounts of power. The Romans had mined every last trace of it, though more for its beauty than magical storage capacity. Most of it was now in the Vatican, guarded like nuclear launch codes, and many magi had fought over possession of even the smallest sliver of the pieces unaccounted for. I never knew how Thaddeus had gotten the ring, but I'd kept it as the spoils of war. I also took a grimoire I doubted I'd need, death powder, and every bullet I had, even the lead ones. I left behind the robes and vestments of my previous life. Regardless of what happened, I wouldn't need them.

Back on the road, I headed north and west to Durango and the crypt. I needed to find out how strong Thaddeus had become since his return. Maybe I could defeat him again, and, this time, make sure he stayed in Hell. Running wasn't an option. I'd seen with my own eyes just how good Thaddeus was at prying a witch out of her lair, and waiting for the inevitable seemed like a miserable existence.

My only choice was to fight.

CHAPTER 4

Sebastian

Final exams aren't supposed to be this hard, I thought as I tried to get the fat warlock into the trunk.

Two days ago, I'd been dropped off in the slums of Phoenix with a sealed envelope and a plastic grocery bag of items. I'd watched the van drive off and walked over to a nearby alley to find out what my mission was and what supplies I'd been given. The sun was just short of setting, the buildings giving off long shadows. Despite the lateness of the day, it was still hot. The streets were deserted, for the most part, but that would change soon enough.

The alley was a bit cooler and well littered with refuse and cast offs. I wended my way carefully—to avoid tripping over anything—and making sure there were no homeless present. My clothes would blend in a bit, but no one would be fooled for long.

I took one more long look up and down the alley then squatted on my heels to see what I had to do. After putting down my bag, I tore open the envelope. Inside was a map, and a printed piece of paper with a grainy picture and instructions underneath. I read the mission brief first.

Daniel Aftowsizi, day trader, 35 years old, single. Lives and works at 23 Crescent circle, Phoenix AZ Makes twice daily trip to barbershop, on corner of Eculid and Baxter, probable front for gambling. Subject is possible warlock. You are to observe him, subdue him, and bring him to All Saints Church, 15 All Saints Drive, Phoenix AZ. Do not cause permanent harm.

After delivery, go to Zola Butte, and get to the top. You have three days.

The map had the house, barbershop, and church all marked for me. The house and barbershop were just ten or twelve blocks apart, but the church was on the other side of town. Neither my current location, nor Zola Butte were marked.

I stared at the photo. I could tell from the image quality it had been taken at a distance and then enlarged and cropped, showing just his upper half and in the background, a barber pole.

Daniel appeared portly with brown hair done in a comb-over. His cheeks sagged, giving him a basset hound look. His eyes were turned away from the camera. He didn't look like a warlock, just some random shlub about to have a really bad day.

I memorized the face, paying attention to the shape of his nose and cheeks, so if he wore a hat or shaved his head, I'd still recognize him. When I had fixed his image in my mind, I wadded up the mission brief and ate it.

Rooting through my bag, I found a can of pepper spray, handcuffs plated in what looked like silver, a ball gag, a pair of gloves, and some electrical tape. I leaned back against the wall and, in a few minutes, had my plan.

After a bit of a search through the debris in the alley, I found my sap—a broken bit of wooden chair leg. I sat back down and carefully wrapped each end with the tape. On one end, I had a nice grip, the other was designed to cushion the impact a little. It's actually quite hard to hit someone in the head with a club and not cause permanent damage, which is why the cops are only supposed to strike arms and legs when subduing a bad guy. A street brawl was out of the question, so a head strike was what I'd have to do, if the pepper spray didn't work.

It took me an hour to figure out where I was and then another two to get to Crescent Circle. By this time, it was fully dark. Taking the bus might've been faster, but as I had no money, it was a foot reconnaissance.

Crescent Circle had seen better days. The houses were small, cheaply-made, single-story units squatting on parched little yards. Two appeared to be foreclosures. There were few lights on in the houses and even fewer yard lights, giving me lots of shadows. Daniel's house was an exception—the porch light was on. I walked past number 23, not looking directly at it, getting a feel for the area. While the neighborhood felt a bit rundown, I didn't get the oily taste of magic. Until I spotted the half-dead cat.

I was squatting in the back of a carport a few houses down from Daniel's place, watching his front door, when I heard a scratching, clawing sound. Not sure if it was a stray dog or something that would give away my position, I froze. From the storm drain in front of the carport, an enormous cat dragged itself onto the street. It was missing the back half of its body and trailing purple-black sparks. Crawling along with just its front legs and claws, it crept toward Daniel's house.

It was halfway across the road when Daniel's door opened, and he stepped outside. "Master," the cat yowled.

Daniel didn't seem to hear the familiar as he closed his door and then waved a hand around. Even though it was dark, the purple-black light of a spell was clearly visible. The door glowed for a second, and Daniel turned back around.

By this time, the cat was almost at his driveway. "Master," the cat called again, and Daniel stiffened a bit until he spotted it.

A slow, sly smile formed on his lips, and he brought his right hand up, snapping his fingers twice. The cat lifted into the air and seemed to soundlessly explode. Daniel walked over to his car, got in, and drove off.

I didn't move for a bit, stunned by what I'd just seen. Daniel was a warlock. Did the Hammers know? Was I being given an impossible task?

Shaking my head to clear it and get back on mission, I remembered my mantra. *I will not fail.*

I left the carport, cut through a few yards and streets until I reached the barbershop.

The shop itself was a long converted shotgun house with a small unlit parking lot on one side. Daniel's car was already there. Walking past the lit window with my head forward, but my eyes turned toward the shop, I looked inside. Only the front third was visible. The back wall had a solid looking door marked "office." There were two barber's chairs, but only one was occupied. Two beefy men sat in plastic chairs, seemingly waiting their turn. They were guards, there to prevent the lucky from actually leaving with their winnings. I crossed the street, and making sure I was in a deep shadow, hunkered down to wait, watching through the window.

Maybe an hour later, Daniel came out holding a fat bank deposit bag. One of the guards started to get up, and Daniel gave him a lazy wave of his free hand. It shimmered purple-black, and the guard stiffened and sat back down.

Really? A Jedi mind trick?

Daniel got into his car and drove off while I thought about what I'd seen. I'd actually learned a lot. Daniel was a scrub, a new warlock. He still cared about money, equating it with power like most rational people. That would change, and soon. His actions with the cat let me know he had something more powerful as a minion. He was turning cruel, mad. It was just a matter of time before he killed, if he hadn't already. His house was warded, and I had no idea what was inside, so an ambush there was out of the question, but here, at the barbershop, that had potential.

The thought of taking on a warlock, even a new one, by myself was worrisome. We went after them in teams, with backup. Yes, I was stronger, better trained, than I had been in New England, but one man Purges weren't done for a reason: we usually lost.

Do I really have a choice?

It took me a long time to come up with a plan that had even a possibility of success. I caught a few hours' sleep then set about gathering supplies. I was in place and ready by nightfall. Waiting there in the dark was the hardest, and I choked down doubts. I'd been given a mission, and I would not fail.

Daniel finally arrived and went inside. I got into position in the unlit parking lot near his car and readied myself. A few minutes later, I heard a commotion and a soft scream. I wanted to rush in and protect the others, but with no real weapons or backup, it was a stupid idea. There was a *whump* as something caught on fire, and a few seconds later, Daniel came out holding a bulging garbage bag.

Using the silver handcuffs as an improvised set of brass knuckles, I swung at him. He must've sensed something coming as he turned slightly, and I ended up rabbit punching him in the side of his neck. I might as well have punched the building; he barely noticed the blow. He stiff-armed me, shoving me back, and I almost left the ground as I flew into the wall of the barbershop. I bounced off it, and my left shoulder screamed in pain at the impact. I choked down a yelp as I steadied myself. Dropping the bag, Daniel turned toward me with a smile as he started to glow purple-black.

He was raising his hands as I fumbled out the soda bottle filled with holy water. I'd poked a hole in the cap so I could use it as a crappy squirt gun. I gave him a long squirt right in his open mouth. He face caught on fire, and he let out a horrific yowl. The flames died out a second later. It had hurt him, but he was still game.

Through a blackened face, he screamed at me, "You're gonna die."

I'd already moved in to finish the fight, and even though he managed to backhand me, nearly taking my head off, I was able to get a cuff on one wrist, and cinch it tight. The silver burned his skin, which smelled like cooking pork, and Daniel, blocked from his power, almost fell over. I pulled the sap from my back pocket and, aiming carefully, swung as hard as I could at the back of his head. The first one didn't faze him much, so I gave him two more, and he slumped down. After rolling him over, I affixed the other cuff with his hands behind his back. Then the ball gag went on, I fished the keys out of his pocket, and opened the trunk of his car.

Dead weight is really hard to move, and it took me what seemed like forever to get him into his trunk. I pulled off his shoes and used the laces to tie his legs together. It wouldn't hold him forever, but maybe it would last long enough.

It took me half the day to find a church so I could scoop some holy water into two discarded soda bottles. I couldn't do a proper Purge, but I could burn down Daniel's house. As I pulled up to the house, I could hear something banging on the front door, trying to get out. Loud booms sounded through the street as something threw itself again and again at the warded door. The door bulged and shook, but didn't open. I put the car in neutral and got out with the remaining bottle. After unscrewing the lid, I dropped it then threw the bottle at the door. Bright blue flames leapt up and quickly started to burn.

"Hey, what's going on?" yelled a neighbor, hanging out of his door. "Oh shit," he exclaimed and ducked back into his house.

I wanted to stay and make sure the minion died, but that was another bad idea. The fire department and cops would be here soon. I ran back to the car and drove off.

* * * *

"What do you mean he's a warlock?" asked Brother Chris. I'd made it back to All Saints Church without being stopped, and gave my report to Brother Chris and Brother Jimmy.

"I saw him do magic. He killed off a cat familiar and had something even bigger in his house. He robbed the barbershop, probably killing everyone inside."

They stared at me for a long moment then Brother Chris said, "Bullshit. Intel checked. They said—" He shook his head. "Bullshit."

Angry, I handed the keys to him. "He's in the trunk. Money's in the car."

While he didn't believe me, Brother Chris didn't take any chances. He put on silvered gauntlets and opened the trunk. The smell of burning flesh wafted out. He reached in with one hand, and I could hear the sizzle from where I stood.

"Holy shit," said Brother Chris as he jerked his hand back and quickly slammed the trunk shut. He turned back and stared at me for a long second then shook his head again. "You two guard him. I'm going to call this in."

I turned to Brother Jimmy. "Can I have a ride to Zola Butte?"

He just nodded, staring at me with wide eyes.

Of course, I didn't get any sleep that night. A hour later, a team pulled up and took over. I was questioned a couple of times, and given a simple purity check.

Brother Jimmy also didn't get any sleep and was cranky. "I can see why they sent you here for more training, but Hammer training is a reward, not a place for troublemakers and screw-ups," he said as he drove. "What did you do that was so great?"

I didn't answer as I figured he didn't really want one; he was just venting.

It all started with a van ride.

CHAPTER 5

Sebastian
15 months ago

When the ceremony was over, we closed up the chapel and loaded into the vans to return to the monastery. I was quiet, and the others mostly left me alone. Objectively, my life was a strange one. I used to be a research chemist, married, and expecting our first child. Jen Riggs, a witch, had changed all that. The cops still think I killed Sarah and burned down our house. Sent to a mental institution for an evaluation, I was given an opportunity to escape, and introduced to the half-hidden world of witches, monsters, and magic. Now I was a monk, trying to stop the evil and damage the power-mad inflicted on the world as best as I could.

Sent to Providence to find Brother James, the area Inquisitor, I'd been chased, captured, tortured, and rescued. I'd even managed to purge a Screwface by myself, and had been given a black ring etched with gold crosses on it as a symbol of my accomplishments. For the first time since entering this new life, I felt like I belonged. That maybe I was competent at my new job. I was fully expecting to be made into a full Inquisitor and given my own area to protect. Unfortunately, Thaddeus, the warlock who'd turned James and commanded him, had followed me. Our trap hadn't been good enough to Purge him, Inquisitors had died, and the survivors had to flee. Now we were headed back to give our report and suffer whatever consequences Bishop Bathoie handed out for failure.

Brother Malachi sat next to me. I'd crossed paths with him a few times, but I could never really fix a mental image of him. I peered intently this time, trying to learn something about the man who was spoken of so respectfully. His hair was short and beginning to gray. He was older than me, maybe even in his early forties, and built wider and shorter.

"This is going to be bad, Sebastian." His light green eyes almost glowed in the reflected light. "We held an unsanctioned mission. Inquisitors died. The answering service was raided, and we lost some good people there. Thaddeus is still at large, and this was the third or fourth time we've fought him and lost. Your exploits are the one good part of this whole debacle. The Bishop is not going to be pleased."

"What's Bishop Bathoie going to do?" I asked. He was not considered a tolerant man.

"No idea. I'm an Inquisitor Plenipotentiary, so he can't touch me, but Brother Walter is in for a bad time."

Damn.

More stuff I didn't know.

This is getting old.

I was supposed to be more than a clueless, nosy research student bumbling along in ignorance. It irritated me, but I asked. "What's an Inquisitor Plenipotentiary?"

His eyes lit up. "It's like a hall pass from the Pope."

Weird. Every other time I'd met or talked with him, he'd been quiet, serious, almost rude. His attitude toward me had changed. I wasn't sure why, but I knew I wasn't just going to float along reacting to things. Even though I was wary, I decided to get more information as he was being friendly.

"Okay," I said, stressing the word to indicate I wanted more.

He gave me a half-smile and a shrug. "It's the ultimate get-out-of-jail-free card. Like being a super Roamer. Roamers have a big district, a state or two they patrol, looking for signs of witchcraft. I do the same thing, only I go wherever. I don't have a district or area. I can access whatever supplies or people I need, and I'm immune from the bishops. They can't assign us duties or discipline. They hate that." He smiled again, raising his hands palms up. "We're seen as loose cannons. If we do something that causes problems in their diocese, they're the ones having to talk to the cardinal."

My eyes went wide, my mouth dropped open.

How can someone be outside the hierarchy?

Brother Malachi continued as though nothing had happened. "Cardinals have little patience for tales of Inquisitors gone wild. We're outside the normal structures, so there are very few of us. Maybe thirty-five in the world. Which is strange. It's not tough to become an Inquisitor Plenipotentiary." A sly smile formed on his scarred face.

He's enjoying this.

So I asked the question he wanted asked. "Tell me, Brother," I said, keeping my face neutral, "how does one become an Inquisitor Plenipotentiary?"

"Commit an act so blindingly stupid others call it brave, save the world, or at least something really important, and have the Pope give you a thumbs up. Do that, you get a fancy title. You also get to wear a pretty ring like mine."

He held up his left hand and showed me the three rings on his middle finger—the one closest to the knuckle was a Hammer ring, gold crosses on it like mine, the middle one was dark purple, and the last jet black. It seemed odd to me that he'd wear them all on the same finger.

"Wait. Pope Benedict gave you a thumbs up?" I said.

"Of course not," he said. "I've never met Pope Benedict. It was Pope John Paul II." He let off a small laugh.

Then it hit me: his ring. He'd dropped his hand, so I had to angle my head a bit, but even in the faint light, I could see it was a carved purple ring. I was sure it wasn't amethyst.

"Brother, is that…?" I trailed off, not sure how to phrase the question.

His smile grew. "Yep. It's porphyrite," he said. "Very rare. The Vatican guards it well. A lot of witches have tried to take it from me. Some by force, others with promises of wealth, power, or even an endless supply of dancing girls." He chuckled. "I'll be honest, the last offer was tempting…but I'm still here."

I was impressed, I'll admit it. I knew he'd actually stopped a lesser demon from being summoned and was regarded with awe, but now—with me, at least—he was funny and even a bit cool.

There's a reason he's acting this way, I warned myself.

"What's the black one for?" His third ring was unlike the others, a dark black that was almost hypnotic.

The smile disappeared, his eyebrows came down and together, and his face flushed and lost all animation. Fists clenched and unclenched, and veins pulsed on his head and neck.

Oh crap. He's gonna attack.

I eased back, trying to get away, to put some distance between us. There was a long tense moment until his face calmed, and he shook his head. I slowly relaxed.

"Sorry," he said, "bad memories." He indicated the ring with a thick finger. "I wear this one out of shame and failure. Maybe I'll tell you about it someday. Now, as for this one," he pointed at his Hammer ring, "make sure you wear yours with a little pride. Not many could Purge a Screwface singlehandedly."

"Brother—"

"Save it," he said, his face once again turning serious. "You earned it, you deserve it, and I don't want to hear any false modesty crap. There are maybe fifty men in North America wearing that ring. Most Hammers die before earning that ring. If nothing else, honor them."

"Yes, Brother," I said, taken a little aback by his sudden change. I was proud that I'd earned the respect of my Brethren, and yet... I shook my head to stop the doubts and recrimination. When I looked back up, he appeared calm. "Next subject. We have to discuss what's going to happen when we get back to the monastery."

I was still shifted away from him, not yet ready to get close, and I had no idea what to say. I needed more information, so I kept my mouth shut and paid attention.

"Like I said, Bishop Bathoie is going to be most displeased with our little mission. He's reporting to the cardinal. I can't imagine it's been a lot of fun for him. Most of his Inquisitors were in Biddeford, Maine, dealing with a necromancer at their medical school. The warlock even went by the name of Herbert West."

I couldn't help smiling—that had to be a joke. "The guy from Reanimator?" I said, chuckling. "Tell me you're pulling my leg?"

His smile had returned. "No, it's true. Not sure where he got the idea. Perhaps he liked the books or the movie, or maybe poor, tortured H.P. was actually onto something." He frowned, and his mouth curled in distaste. "The problem for the bishop is that he didn't know what we were doing. No leader likes to learn about events after they occur, and when people die, it's even worse."

"Well, I understand protocol and all, but what about exigent circumstances?"

He barked a laugh. "Sebastian," he said, "we're Inquisitors, not cops. We weren't defending ourselves. We conducted an unsanctioned mission. It'll look like he's lost control. That we're going rogue. If he's not in charge, if he can't keep us in line, the cardinal will wonder why he has a bishop. Or, at least, this particular bishop."

Still wary of his motivation, I didn't know what to say. It was absurd and futile to second-guess highly trained people, weighing them down with rules that only made sense in calm reflection. There was a place for them, but not when magic and bullets were flying.

"I'll take responsibility, of course," he said. "However, the bishop will want his pound of flesh, and that will be Brother Walter. The bishop was tasked with the Purge of Thaddeus and has failed so far. He's not going to be in a forgiving mood. Brother Walter will likely be the scapegoat. "

I frowned. How could Brother Malachi be so callous? Brother Walter had saved my life, tried to make me laugh when I was wounded and in the hospital. He'd stood with me in battle, and I owed him.

"We can explain what happened, that I was being tracked by the bone needle, that we had to stop them," I said.

Brother Malachi shook his head. "Sebastian, we failed. We didn't Purge Thaddeus. We gave it our best shot, and we failed. Good intentions count for little. It's what you accomplish in this life that matters."

"So we're just going to offer up Brother Walter as a sacrifice?"

He frowned in turn. "Don't be a child. What you need to do is report exactly what happened, nothing more and nothing less. This won't be a normal debrief, it'll be an inquest. A way to fix blame." He peered intently into my eyes, making his point. "Don't get emotional. It'll be used against you. Keep your answers short, don't offer opinions. Don't speculate. Don't let them draw you into open-ended questions. If asked what you would do differently, say 'nothing.' Most importantly, don't try to offer yourself up in his place." He shook his head slowly. "It won't help Brother Walter, and it will hurt you."

"But—"

Brother Malachi slapped a hand down on the seat. "I'm telling you what to do to help everyone, including Brother Walter. If you go off half-cocked, if you try to find justice or attempt a verbal rescue, you'll be in a world of hurt. Don't make this worse by acting up. Your antics as an apprentice won't help you. What you've done, the cleansing of Providence, the Purging of the witches, facing Thaddeus, that's what matters here."

He was right, but it felt like I was abandoning the others. Letting them down somehow.

"Now," he said, suddenly changing the subject, "I'm going to get some sleep. I suggest you do the same."

I tried, but there was no way I could sleep after hearing what Brother Malachi had said. His plan felt wrong. Maybe he was correct, but it seemed cowardly, as though we were abandoning one of our own. I still didn't see why he was bothering with me, why he thought I had a role to play in this. I tried to determine his motives, but nothing came to mind.

CHAPTER 6

When we pulled up to the main house of the monastery, there was none of the usual happiness and relief that Brothers had survived. Our reception committee stood like a row of angry crows on a wire. The abbot was there, and Brother John, my first mentor, with ten or fifteen monks. Glaring at us from the back of the group was Bishop Bathoie. His mouth was just a slit across his face, his brow furrowed in anger and concentration. No words were spoken. Or needed.

When I got out of the van, I was ready to lash out at the hostility. I'd done my part. Why was anyone acting shitty to me? Brother Malachi put a hand on my arm, and when I looked back, gave me a small shake of his head.

Fine. We'll do it his way. For now.

I was calm but not meek. I'd done nothing wrong.

We were separated and given a purity ritual—a quick check to make sure the person hasn't been corrupted. Mine was done by a monk I'd never seen before. After I was cleared, he tried to get me to leave my gear with the van.

"No," I told him, not with the anger I felt, but as a fact. They could play their games, trying to make me feel guilty, but I wasn't buying into it. The picture of me and my wife on our wedding day was still in my backpack, and I was not about to lose it again. Glancing around, I spotted Brother John.

I walked over to him and handed him my gear and weapon. "Could you take care of this?"

Brother John nodded, his normally placid face lined with concern and sorrow. I paused to ask him what was going on, but he shook his head at me.

I was escorted by two monks to the classroom building, and then into a small room I'd never seen before. We passed a table holding a variety of sandwiches, water, and an enormous bowl of fruit. My stomach rumbled, but I didn't get a chance to stop. The room was mostly empty and looked like an interrogation room from TV. There were only two chairs and a table in it, and another monk waiting for me.

"My name is Brother Mike," he said as my escort left. "We're going to be here awhile, so would you like some water or something to eat?"

"Yes," I said, "a cheeseburger and water would be nice." I was hungry and saw no need to take my frustration out on some stranger, but it was tempting. Right on cue, the doubts I thought I'd left behind boiled up.

You're so screwed. Confess to everything, and maybe they'll let you stay.

When Brother Mike knocked, the door opened, and he went out. There was no doorknob on this side. I was a prisoner. Four cameras were mounted high in the corners. I thought about giving them a show, tossing some furniture around, or at least flipping them off, but, instead, I sat down and waited. I looked calm, but inside I was fuming.

A few minutes later, Brother Mike returned with my food, a big bottle of water, a legal pad, and some pens. He handed me the food and waited for me to finish.

Trying to be polite, I started off the conversation. "What questions do you have for me, Brother?"

Short and thin, Brother Mike had a narrow, pointed face. His blond hair seemed to think that growing in several different directions at the same time was fashionable. He didn't give off the aura of a field Inquisitor, but had a distinct bureaucrat vibe.

You're just trying to hate him because you're guilty.

I sighed inwardly. I wasn't ready for another mental fight with myself. Moving away from things that might be my fault, I concentrated on my treatment since I'd returned to the monastery, working up a self-righteous anger.

Dammit, I thought, *I've done nothing wrong. Why are they treating me like this? Because you deserve it, and more.*

My self-flagellation was interrupted by Brother Mike. "If you would, please tell me what's happened to you since you arrived in Providence."

That was about as polite as you could ask for. Feeling like a real ass, I abandoned my little mental war and described, again, what had happened to me since I got that call from Brother Otto.

It took a long time, and I had to stop to collect myself or take a drink, but Brother Mike never interrupted me or tried to speed me up. He just waited patiently, and took the occasional note. It still hurt, but at least now the end was, "and I made it back safe to the monastery."

Brother Mike looked at me for a very long time when I was done. Finally, he said, "That was most impressive, Brother."

Creeping warmth rose from my collar and my face flushed. I'd spent most of my time running away or being beaten up, not being heroic. "Thanks," I muttered.

"There are going to be a lot of questions, and it will take me a while to gather them all." He reached into a pocket and pulled out a slim leather-bound book, which he passed to me. "This is my missal. Feel free to read it while I'm away. I pray this will not take long."

His words sounded formulaic and put me at ease.

He's just doing his job.

I thanked him and opened it.

Something that looked like the outline of a demonic octopus glowed at me in a purple-black light. The image was wrong, with lines that were straight and curved at the same time. It moved, squirmed. My eyes watered. I wanted to look away, but I was transfixed. Sound nagged at the edge of my hearing, like a friend calling me from far away. A cruel, laughing voice whispered promises, suggestions, and possible futures. My stomach heaved, and my dinner came up messily. I fell off the chair onto my side and curled up, vomit and bile running out the side of my mouth. The image pounded and clawed at my brain. Someone picked me up and cleaned the vomit off. My shirt was removed and another forced on. I was maneuvered back into my chair, and by the time I could refocus, the door was being closed, and it was just me and Brother Mike again. The room smelled of industrial cleanser and vomit.

"Sorry about that," said Brother Mike, "we had to be sure you were still pure, without taint."

"Could've asked," I said, trying to ignore my rumbling stomach and the taste in my mouth. I grabbed the water bottle and took several deep gulps that didn't help. My anger started to come back, but I was too weak to do much more than sit and sip my water.

"Do you really think we could've trusted your answer?" he said. "You were held for several days by Thaddeus and James. Tortured. You say you didn't break, but who would admit to that? They performed magic on you, messed with your memories and brain. Brother Paul cut d a bone needle out of you. Perhaps it was in long enough to turn you, a subtle taint waiting for the right moment to erupt. We didn't know. So we tested you, just to be sure." He gave me a big smile and stuck out his hand. "Welcome home, Brother."

I shook it. I didn't want to—I wanted to bounce him off the walls—but I shook his damn hand. "So are we done here? Is my interrogation over?"

He looked pained. "I'm sorry, Brother, but I wasn't here to question you. It was my job to make sure you hadn't been turned. Someone else will handle the official debrief."

The blood drained out of my face, my vision narrowed, and my heart sped up. "What did you say?" I stood up, ready to turn this smug little turd into bite-sized pieces of monk. "You've been fucking with me for hours, and that's not my official debrief?"

Brother Mike shot out of his chair and backed toward the door. He was saying something, but I wasn't listening. I moved around the table toward him. The door opened, and he slid out before I could get to him.

Brother Otto strode in. He had a look on his face I'd never seen before: anger and disgust. "Sebastian," he yelled. "What is wrong with you? I'm tired of your whiny, 'poor me' attitude. You will answer every question asked of you, you will assist in any way asked of you, and you will run the hills as penance and think about ways to control that temper of yours." His words hit me like a bucket of cold water.

I froze, half-crouched, embarrassed and ashamed of what I'd just done.

Brother Otto pointed at my chair. "Now sit down and behave. The bishop expects your full cooperation, and so do I, and so does Brother Malachi."

That made me pause on my way back to my chair.

What did he mean by that?

Brother Otto was standing in the doorway, hands on his hips, his face full of anger. Then he winked at me. It was a twitch, so fast the cameras would never catch it. Brother Otto was telling me something. It took me a second, and then I remembered Brother Malachi's warning.

"Don't get emotional. Don't speculate."

He was trying to prepare me for this. Maybe.

43

I understood at least enough for right now. I sat back down, and, thinking meek thoughts, apologized for my actions and promised to help in any way asked.

Brother Otto gave me a quick nod and closed the door behind him.

CHAPTER 7

A few minutes later, a different monk came in. He looked like the Inquisitor version of the White Rabbit from Alice in Wonderland.

"My name is Brother Geoffrey, that's with a 'G' not a 'J.' I'm the special assistant to Bishop Bathoie, and you, monk, are in a lot of trouble." He said this all in a rush as he put down another pad of paper and more pens, but remained standing.

I was actually open-mouthed at his audacity. By calling me 'monk' instead of 'Brother,' he was trying to intimidate me. Or something. As he stood right at five and a half feet and weighed maybe a hundred and fifty pounds, his attempt to cow me didn't work. I tried to keep the smile off my face as I offered him my hand. He reminded me of a man I'd known long ago—a petty bureaucrat at the DMV, enraged at how his life had turned out, who used his tiny allotment of power vindictively.

"Nice to meet you, Brother," I said, trying to be pleasant. I was still a bit embarrassed over losing my temper earlier. "How can I help you?"

He ignored my hand and stood there, his nostrils actually flaring a little as he gave me what I guessed was his 'Inquisitor' face.

This has to be a joke. There's no way this guy's for real.

Even the dark part of my brain—always ready to mock me, to tell me what I've done wrong or why I'm a failure—was silent in awe of this pompous display. I lowered my hand and asked him again how I could help him.

He finally got tired of his bad impression of a tough guy. "You will tell me everything you've seen or done since you received Brother Otto's phone call directing you to locate Brother James."

"I've given my debrief several times. Should I give you the highlights, or maybe tell you what's happened recently?"

"Start from the beginning, monk," he said.

"You didn't get to watch the debriefs, or at least read the transcripts?"

He looked angry for a second, so clearly he hadn't seen anything. He knew nothing. Brother Geoffrey wasn't a player; he was an errand boy, a desk-riding, paper-pushing cube monkey. He'd been sent in here to be a pain or get some reaction from me.

Fine. I can play this game.

"Of-of course I have," he lied, stammering over the words. "Just do as I instruct."

Suppressing my desire to screw with him, I told my story again, keeping it short and to the point. I left off some things, like my seeing my wife again, but the rest of it was more or less accurate.

He interrupted me every few minutes with long, rambling questions, most of them pointless. I figured he was trying to irritate me, so I irritated him by not reacting, and using my hearing loss as an excuse to get him to repeat everything at least twice.

"Are you trying to be obtuse, monk?" he demanded once.

"No, Brother," I said, "as you know from my file, I've had some hearing loss and it sometimes makes it difficult for me to understand nuanced questions."

"So you're no longer capable of the duties you've been assigned?" he said.

"I'm undergoing medical treatment at the moment, but so far I've been able to do everything fine," I said, after having him repeat the question.

This went on for hours. I would retell my tale, and he'd interrupt with some pointless interjection. I would have him repeat it, and then finally respond in a calm, detached manner. I referenced my prior debriefs often—"as you know from my earlier debrief," or, "if you remember, from reading my debrief"—to further irritate him. It worked. He had a habit of running his hands through his hair, and by the time I was done, it was sticking up in various places, and his face was red and sweaty.

46

"What are your questions?" I said when I'd completed my tale yet again.

"Tell me again," he said.

"Tell you what again?" I asked.

"Start over and tell me everything."

"You want me to repeat what I just said?"

His face went from red to purple, and his hands clenched in poorly-suppressed anger. "Monk," he said, his voice louder, "you will do as I bid and tell me your story from the beginning."

"Of course, Brother. I just thought you were listening to me," I said.

"I was listening. I want you to tell me your story again."

"Oh, I understand. You have a comprehension problem." I gave him a sad look. "I'm sorry. I didn't realize you're differently-abled. I'll speak slower for you, and use smaller words." I never got to finish mocking him. I'd hit a button, and it enraged him.

He stood up, banging his fists on the table. "I'm not disabled," he said very loudly, shouting at me with spittle flying. His face was the color of an eggplant and foam formed in the corners of his mouth.

I didn't react. I kept my face as calm as possible, but inside I felt a big smile.

He loomed over me, shouting some more, and it looked like he was going to hit me.

My plan was to let him have one punch and then tie him up in a pretzel.

The door opened and a loud voice called out, "Brother Geoffrey, come here now."

He froze for a second, lowered his hands, and turned away. The door closed behind him. I made very sure not to smile, but it was hard.

A little bit later, the door opened again, and a familiar face came in with another cheeseburger and water.

"Brother Thomas," I said, "it's good to see you again." It was good to see him, but I was still wary.

Careful, I reminded myself. This could be another trap.

Thomas and I had come up together. He'd gone into Intel and spent his time assisting with the prep work for a Purge, recruiting, and manning the 'emergency help' line.

In order to become an Inquisitor, an apprentice has to Put a witch to the Question. He has to torture her. Nothing else works to get their information, contacts, and grimoire. A grimoire is the source of a witch's knowledge. She

47

treasures it above all things other than her life; without it, she can't perform complex spells or learn anything new. She would be weak and easy prey for others of her kind.

It's rumored that if an apprentice fails, if he can't or won't take this final noxious step, he's summarily executed. It's a terrible, soul-staining ordeal, and at the time, I really wasn't sure I could go through with it. I was ready to walk out of that barn and accept the bullet. Even though I knew what she'd done. Even though I'd seen the eyeballs in glass jars, the animals she'd broken so completely they wanted to die. Thomas was my assistant and helped me, forced me, to do what I had to do. I loved and hated him for that.

He gave me the cheeseburger and water. "Here. You've got to be hungry. I'll talk, you eat." I looked at it and then him for a long second and dug in.

I'd forgotten how hungry I was until Thomas brought in the food.

I was halfway through before he opened his mouth. "First off," he said, "congratulations. You've become a gold ring Hammer, Purged a Screwface by yourself...that's incredible. Also, you've passed the anger test."

"The what?" I said, between bites.

"The anger test. Do you remember what distinguishes normal people from the ones who can become a witch?"

I swallowed the last bite and thought for a second before shaking my head.

He looked kind of surprised. "Think. What deficit does a person have to have in order to become a witch?"

I gave it a thought then went for the answer he seemed to want. "Anger."

"Not only anger, but rage, the inability to stop being angry. Most people get angry, and it goes away. Some people nurture their anger, feed it until it controls them, until it becomes rage. Those are the Inquisitors we have to watch out for, the people we can't become. When you snapped at Brother Mike, we were concerned, but Brother Otto calmed you down. Maybe it was a normal reaction, maybe there was a problem. We sent Brother Geoffrey in to check. You were able to handle that without an issue. You even managed to make him angry and didn't respond."

"Oh, so that 'monk' crap was an act?"

"Yep. He's in Intel with me. He's a master at pretending to be different kinds of people. He does the petty functionary really well. Never play poker with him. He'll clean you out. He's the one we send out to make money at the casinos when we need some."

I mulled this over for a minute. "So are we done here?"

Thomas grimaced a little. "No. There are some questions we need answered. Not fun ones. They're about when you saw Sarah."

"Oh." I wasn't sure what to say. I really didn't want to talk about my wife.

"You've said in several debriefs that you saw her again when you were being held. When Thaddeus and James were torturing you. Correct?"

"Yes." I wasn't sure where this was going. Maybe they thought I was crazy. Maybe I was still being tested.

You probably are crazy, and this is just another test.

"How did she look? Like a person, like herself, or something else?"

"What do you mean?" I asked.

"Did she look like she'd been," he paused, probably choosing his words carefully, "injured? Like the last time you saw her?"

Thomas was dancing around it, but I knew what he meant. Did she look like she'd been brutally murdered? Thrown through a window and allowed to bleed to death, in pain and alone? Did she look scared, not only for her life but also for her unborn child? Realizing as her life flowed out of her that I wouldn't be there. I wouldn't save her. That I'd failed in my most basic role as husband—that of protector.

I closed my eyes and took a deep breath, both to keep from screaming and to remember. I unclenched my fists, let out the breath, and slowly opened my eyes.

"At the time, I didn't really pay attention to anything but the fact that she was there. Thinking back on it, she looked like she did before she became pregnant, but sometimes she would become a bit transparent. Every now and then I could see what was behind her a little."

"Sarah was an apparition? Not solid, but transparent. Like you'd expect a ghost to be?"

"Yes."

"How did she look? What was her expression?"

"She seemed calm. Serene. I thought she forgave me. That she was there to take me with her, that it was finally over." I stopped before the blurring in my eyes became too much.

Thomas politely looked down at his notes for a moment. "So she was calm, unwounded, and transparent?"

"Yes."

"But at the same time, she wasn't real? She was an abstract? A stylized version of herself?"

49

I thought hard about this for a moment, doubts and fractured memories whizzing around inside my mind. "No. She looked like she did about six months before she died."

"Why?"

"Dunno. Maybe that when she was happiest, maybe... I dunno."

"Have you seen her spirit before you were captured?"

"No."

"Have you seen Sarah since then?" he asked.

"The last time I saw Sarah was when Thaddeus put a copper wire into my skull. He burned out part of my brain. Sarah stopped moving, shattered into pieces, and disappeared." It hurt to say it.

"No other time? Not before, not after, not now?"

'No, just then. Brother Scott thought it was important, but I don't know why."

"It's unusual, that's all," he said calmly, but Thomas and I had trained together for months; I knew he was keeping something back. I kept staring at him, and he broke, "Okay, it's really strange. Not 'lock Sebastian up, he's gone crazy,' but...something...different. You saw a...um," he paused, clearly searching for the right word. "You've seen...a ghost, for lack of a better term."

"So?" I prompted.

"Well, Brother Fred has been doing debriefs for twelve years, and he's never had someone report a ghost."

Brother Fred was the one who'd visited me in the asylum. He'd given me the choice: stay and be convicted of killing my wife, or come with him for a chance to kill the witch who'd framed me. Neither of which had happened. Yes, Jen Riggs was dead, and at my hand, but not in the way I'd hoped for, not in a Purge, but as an act of mercy that haunted me.

"Brother Fred's old. He has to have been an Inquisitor longer than twelve years." I was stalling, trying to change the subject while I thought.

Thomas smiled. "Nice try. Brother Fred had a leg clawed. It's tough for him to run far or fast. So he joined Intel." He paused for a moment, looking me straight in the eye. "Would you please tell me again, the part when you saw Sarah? What was happening, what she looked like, what she did?"

So I told him about the torture, the time she appeared and shushed me, when she watched me, and then when she died. It was difficult to recall those memories, to relive what had happened. She was there with me, just for a little while, and losing her a second time was even worse than the first.

50

"She never spoke to you?"

"Not a word. She...she watched. I guess."

"Why do you think she was there?"

I took another deep cleansing breath and stilled myself. When I was ready, I spoke. "The first time, I thought she was there to take me to heaven. James had killed me—he said an aneurism had burst, that I was dying—and she showed up. She walked through the wall and stood there."

"Wait," said Thomas. "You think you died?"

I shrugged. "I felt a pop in my head and started to black out. James did... I dunno— He did a spell, I guess. Something dark and evil crept through me, and after a minute, I was fine. Sarah was still there. James looked like he'd cast a spell. He was tired and still had the afterglow. You know, there was a purple-black aura about him that faded out after a second or two. Looked like he did magic to me. He told me an aneurysm had burst, and he'd saved me. No idea if it was true."

"Why would a warlock save you?"

"He told me he was supposed to break me, turn me into his dog, so he couldn't let me die."

"When did you see her next?"

"James took away the pain of beating me for a while and had two witches talk to me at the same time." I shivered with the memory. "That was bad. I thought I was going to lose it. I couldn't ignore what they were saying, and I couldn't focus on only one voice. Trying to listen to two was scrambling my mind."

"Dichotomous aural input," he said, his face screwed up as though he was trying to remember the phrase. "It's what happens when you try to focus on two different, competing sounds at the same time. The brain can't process it, can't ignore it. Eventually insanity ensues or the brain shuts down."

"Okay, well they did that for an hour, supposedly. James threatened to beat me again, and that's when Sarah came through the ceiling and shushed me."

"Why'd she do that, do you think?"

"No idea. Maybe she was trying to tell me not to talk. Maybe she was letting me know she was there. I don't know."

"And did anyone else see her? Did she interact with anyone or anything?"

"Not that I could tell. Sarah walked right past a witch once, and the witch didn't really react."

Thomas peered intently at me. "What do you mean she didn't really react?"

"Well, she didn't move or anything, but she wrinkled up her nose like she'd smelled something bad. I didn't think much of it. I was looking at Sarah, and the reaction could've been from anything."

Thomas looked pensive and remained silent for a while.

Finally, I asked, "What's it mean, Brother Thomas? I'm not crazy…at least, I don't think so. Was it just signs and portents without meaning?"

Thomas shook his head. "I don't think you're crazy, but I don't know what it means either. It could be anything or nothing." The silence stretched out, and then, coming to some internal decision, Thomas said, "Last few questions. Did you know anything about the unauthorized mission?"

"No. Brother Paul told me they were worried about the bone needle, so they kept that information from me until it was removed."uu

"If you'd known, would you have gone with them?"

I paused for a moment then lied, remembering Brother Malachi's warnings. "No."

"What do you think should happen to Brothers who perform unsanctioned missions?"

"I'm not in a position to judge, and I don't have the details of what happened. There's no way I could honestly speculate on that."

Thomas gave me a sharp look, and waited. He was letting the silence tempt me into talking more.

I stared back at him and said nothing. Inside I felt both sad and a bit angry. They'd used a friend, someone I'd trust, to try to get me to sell out Brother Walter.

We stayed that way for what seemed like hours until he must've realized I wasn't going to say anything else.

"Very well, Sebastian, we're done here. You are confined to the monastery until this situation is resolved. Bishop Bathoie is conducting a thorough review, and you are expected to assist in any way you can."

"Of course," I said.

CHAPTER 8

The next few days went by in semi-isolation. The first day I avoided everyone, still angry about how I'd been treated, how my Brothers had tried to manipulate me. When I went to see Brother John about getting my gear back, he told me it had been confiscated by the Bishop. The picture might get me in a little trouble, but it would be worth it to me. I liked being able to see Sarah's smiling face to keep her memory alive. The isolation depressed me, and I was treated like a leper—people actually ducked away from me, and there was no one to talk to about what was going on, at least no one I trusted not to use my loneliness against me.

The Residence, where I had my own room, filled up with other Inquisitors quickly, but my hours were spent alone. Nightmares plagued my sleep—some formless, just bare emotions of terror and helplessness, others detailed and disturbing—which led to me keeping odd hours, avoiding Mass as much as I could, and going for long runs around the monastery. The first run was penance for my anger, but then I started running to kill time and wear myself out enough to sleep. I was still recovering from what James and Thaddeus had done to me, and my pace was slow and labored. My initial run consisted of more walking than running, completely stopping for rest every couple of miles.

I skipped most meals—I wasn't that hungry—even though in Residence you're expected to attend the meals, not only for the food and Bible readings but also the silent fellowship that occurs when breaking bread with your Brethren.

A couple of times I was summoned back to the "interrogation room," as I mentally called it, and asked a few questions. Some were clarification, others attempts to get me to condemn the action of others, or to speculate on what I might do "if." I kept my answers short and factual. I refused to be drawn into accusations or speculation.

On the fourth or fifth day of this, I visited the firing range under the classroom building. My pistol had been recovered when I was rescued and ended up back at the monastery before I did.

"Are you ready to qualify, Brother Sebastian?" said Brother Rodger, our weapons master.

"I'd like to make sure before I run the actual table, see if I need some practice," I said.

He just nodded and walked off. He was never a talkative man, and when teaching, could be very strict. This time, however, he seemed to be keeping his distance.

I did a couple of practice runs. My unofficial scores were acceptable, so I set up the tables for qualification. When it was over, I had a new personal best. Brother Rodger, who did the scoring and time-keeping, did so without comment. His mood killed my pleasure over my minor success.

When I got back to the Inquisitors' Residence, I had a couple of people waiting for me. The common room for apprentices was set up like a fraternity common room, minus the alcohol. Near-white walls and a highly polished linoleum floor gave it a bright, cheery atmosphere. There was a big TV, flanked by comfortable couches and chairs, a pool table, and a poker table, where we bet chores instead of money. To me, it had a restful and masculine feel. Dark wood paneling surrounded the Inquisitors' common room, arranged to cater to solitude or small groups. There were lots of high-backed chairs, with nearby end tables. One wall was taken up by a bookshelf that held everything from Bibles and missals to weapons manuals. A grandfather clock ticked away in one corner. Coffee, tea, and other drinks were available from the staff.

I'm still waiting for the day I walk into the Inquisitors' common room and there'll be pipe smoke and men wearing deerstalker hats, saying things like "I say, old chap," and "jolly good." I doubt you'd see that in a real English gentleman's club—I probably get my ideas from reading too much Sherlock Holmes—but still...

A part of our meager salary was docked to pay a couple of semi-retired Inquisitors to run it for us. We don't really make money, as we are the "Poor Brothers," it's just a small stipend so that we can travel when needed or for emergencies. Most of it's taken up by expenses, and the rest goes back into our retirement fund.

Just inside the front door of the Inquisitors' Residence was a desk manned by Brother Giuseppe, who had to be in his seventies. He was in charge of the Residence; we just stayed there from time to time. Occasionally, he would ask for a small favor, and whether it was taking out the trash or stealing something from the Library of Congress, Inquisitors stopped everything and did it. If an Inquisitor needed something, or wanted information through different channels, they'd go see him, and it would be done. Brother Giuseppe had been around so long, knew where so many bodies were buried, and was so well connected that everyone deferred to him.

"Brother Sebastian," he said when I walked in, "two things. First, you have visitors in the common room. Second, let me see that ring I've been hearing about."

I walked over to him and offered my left hand, which he took in both of his. They were old and liver-spotted, but still strong.

He leaned close and peered at my ring, mumbling to himself. Still holding my hand, he looked back up at me. "Well done, Brother. I fought the Lord's enemies for forty years—forty long years—before I took this Majordomo job, and I've never been of the caliber to Purge a Screwface. And to do it by yourself..." He paused for a beat. "It is quite extraordinary." He gave my hand a pat and let it go.

I felt pleased by this praise. "Thank you, Brother." I stood there for a second, squirming like a little kid waiting for more.

"Best go see your visitors. You can tell me about it later."

"Yes, Brother," I said and went into the common room.

There are no official rules, as such, just informal ones handed down from Inquisitor to Inquisitor. These guidelines make sense; no one wants loud conversations while trying to relax or concentrate on disassembling a Colt 1911. No one wants to smell the results of someone's five mile run or their time in the hand-to-hand combat pit. I'd just come from the range, and smelled a little of burnt gunpowder, and I risked silent criticism from the others. I could've washed up first or even taken a quick shower, but I really wanted to talk with someone about what was going on. I hadn't seen Brother Otto, my mentor, since he admonished me for yelling at Brother Mike.

It wasn't Brother Otto, but Brothers Maurice and Malachi. Maurice was another classmate from my apprentice days. He'd come to training fat and a little off, mentally. Now he was heavily muscled, built like a small linebacker, and very off. He learned fast and was as dangerous as a drunken Viking. He was also my friend. I hadn't seen him since the hospital, where he'd almost gotten into a gunfight with the Hammers giving me a field debrief. He probably would've won.

They were sitting in a small cluster of chairs around a table, talking quietly. A few other Inquisitors were there, giving them a wide berth, mostly reading. One large Hammer seemed to be asleep. They saw me coming across the room and stood when I reached them. We gave each other one-armed man hugs and sat down.

"It's good to see you both," I said, starting things off. "What's up?"

"We're just plotting how to take over the snack food market and control the US via junk food. Wanted to know if you were in or not," said Maurice.

That put a much-needed smile on my face.

"We're here to see you, you idiot. See how things are going for you."

Brother Malachi just nodded in agreement.

"Well, I have a few extra question sessions, some follow up. They tried to get me to play 'if' games, but I kept my answers short and didn't go there. I couldn't really give an honest answer to one of those anyway." I said this for their benefit and for anyone else who might be listening. I was feeling a bit paranoid.

"Like I said, be honest, and help in any way asked," said Brother Malachi. It was only a small part of what he'd told me in the van, but I got the hint. I was still a bit wary, but his instructions were spot on. He'd been right when he'd warned me what to expect and how to react.

Things would probably be a real mess had he not told you what to say and how to act.

"So let's see this ring of yours, Mister Screwface-slayer," said Maurice. He took my hand and 'oohed' and 'aahed' extravagantly. He looked at me, his dark eyes dancing, and said, "Now let me get this right. You walked into a Hoodoo shop, on some religious quest to root out evil in Providence. You were accosted by a really ugly woman, who you shot without provocation. It took you a full magazine of ammo before you actually hit her and then you burned down her store to cover your crime? And for this they gave you a ring? Doesn't seem right." He turned to Brother Malachi. "Since I'm a real witch hunter, and can actually hit what I aim at, unlike this sorry Red Sox fan, does that mean I get a ring as well?"

We all laughed, and I made sure Maurice saw my one-finger response.

"How are you doing, Sebastian?" asked Brother Malachi once we'd stopped.

The question caught me off guard, and I spilled out my anger and frustration to them. "You're the only visitors I've had. I haven't seen Brother Otto since the first day. I gave Brother John my gear, but I don't have it back yet. I only saw Thomas as he was part of my debrief. Brother Rodger barely spoke to me at the range. I feel so isolated. It's like I've done something wrong. I've gone over what happened in my head a dozen times, and I can't think of anything I did to expose us, or bring shame, or...or fail in some way." I suddenly realized how much what was going on hurt and shut up, as I had no desire to become a weepy wreck.

They looked at each other, and Brother Malachi gave Maurice a small nod.

"Sebastian," Maurice said, "do you remember when we were apprentices?"

"Yes," I said slowly, giving him a sideways glance.

"You and Rubin were goofing off in class one day, so Brother Otto gave you that mission to plan. Then Thomas helped out, and Brother Otto was so impressed with what you guys did, he excused you from Planning class and took you out on a mission."

I turned to face him directly, my brow furrowed. "Yes, so? We all had to get missions to matriculate. It was easy for us as Brother Otto was in residence and could take us along anytime he had a mission."

"True," Maurice said slowly. "But other apprentices had been here longer. The Inquisitors they were paired with were somewhere else. They had to scramble even to get on missions. There were only so many available, and some had waited for months. They thought they were supposed to be next. Worse, they were still stuck in Planning. You guys got out of the class in a week."

I nodded, still not sure what Maurice was angling at.

"How about Brother Fergus?" he asked. "That really big guy from England? Remember how he reacted when he found out you guys were going?"

"Yes." I nodded. Actually Brother Fergus was mad because we'd talked Brother Otto into taking Maurice. He hadn't done any of the work, but Apprentice Roamers needed more training—five missions instead of the usual three. When Brother Otto left, Brother Fergus and a few others, seeing we were going on a mission, got upset. Rubin and Fergus were almost face-to-face, shouting at each other over the "fairness" of what had happened. For a moment, I'd thought fists were going to start flying.

"What was the reason Rubin gave for the hostility?" asked Maurice.

"Jealousy," I said. "Brother Fergus and the others were mad because Thomas and I got out of Planning for doing a good job on that assignment."

"Same thing here," said Maurice.

"Huh?"

Maurice rolled his eyes and looked over to Brother Malachi. "Help me make him understand."

Brother Malachi smiled. "I already told you there are very few Hammers who've ever Purged a Screwface by themselves. In all of North America, there are only a few dozen wearing our ring. Well, here you are, not even a fully vested Inquisitor, without Hammer training, and you Purge a Screwface by yourself. You did something that Inquisitors with ten or fifteen years of experience have never done, and may not be capable of doing."

"Oh," I said.

"Sebastian, we may be monks, but we're still men. Petty, vain, prone to jealousy, and all the rest. You made them feel small by doing what they cannot. It'll take them a while to adjust, and some may never. How do you think Brother Otto feels right now about what happened to you?"

"He told me he thought it was a simple mission," I said.

"Partly true," said Brother Malachi. "I'm sure he does feel guilty for sending you out to Providence with all that happened, but at the same time, look at what you did. How you excelled at every turn. No instructor wants to be outshined by their student. Yes, there's pride in helping someone grow, but there's also a little resentment if everyone focuses on the student and not the teacher."

I sat back in my chair, stunned. I didn't think I'd done anything special.

So now even Brother Otto hates you. I crammed a knuckle into my eye socket, pushing hard.

"Don't worry," said Brother Malachi. "Brother Otto's a good man. He just needs to sort out a few things. Mostly he needs your forgiveness."

"What?" I said, giving the two of them a confused look, leaning forward again. "Forgiveness for what? He thought it was an easy mission. He warned me to be careful. No one could've expected Thaddeus. You guys came and rescued me. I made it out okay, I guess. I mean other than...well..." I waved my hand toward my head.

"Have you told him that?" asked Maurice.

"No. I haven't had the chance."

"Make sure you do," said Brother Malachi.

58

We sat there in silence for a few minutes, until the grandfather clock started to chime. Other Inquisitors began to rise and leave the common room.

"Dinner time," said Maurice, rubbing his hands together.

CHAPTER 9

A lot of heads turned when we walked in.

"Relax," said Maurice when I slowed down. "They're just admiring me."

Brother Malachi snorted.

The dining hall was large with a vaulted ceiling. The high table was opposite the door we'd come through, and three long tables were perpendicular to it. Normally half-full, tonight the hall was busy. The Benedictines we shared the monastery with sat together at the far right table. The middle table and most of the left were full of Inquisitors in their gray robes and apprentices in their brown robes with gray stitching.

"I don't see any of our novices," said Maurice as we collected our trays.

I looked around, but didn't spot anyone wearing the plain brown robes indicating novice status.

"Perhaps they're trying to leave a duck at a poker table. Hope they don't go beating up innocent mobsters," said Brother Malachi.

I flushed red while Maurice asked, "You heard about that?"

Brother Malachi nodded with a smile. "Everyone knows about that little incident."

At the high table, the abbot was joined by Bishop Bathoie, the librarian, and a few others I didn't recognize. The abbot stood up and began with an announcement.

"Before the blessing, I must point out that the Poor Brothers will need the hall for the next day or so. They are conducting some internal matters. The hall will be off limits to the rest of the monastery until the Poor Brothers have completed their work. Meals will be upstairs, and the Poor Brothers have offered to have pizza delivered for the inconvenience, which I think is more than fair."

Watching the other monks rather than the abbot, I spotted a lot of monks glancing at each other; pizza was a rare treat.

The abbot continued, "Cardinal Reynolds will also be attending, to observe and do a review of our work here. I expect everyone to be on their best behavior."

The abbot blessed the food, and I picked at my salad.

Finally, I thought, *this will be over and I can get back to being an Inquisitor. Maybe.*

That night, I was able to sleep, for a change, and the next morning came quickly. Brother Malachi, Maurice, and I stuck together once we were up. Breakfast was some eggs on a paper plate, and juice served upstairs in the main hall. When it was over, Maurice grumbled that he'd been hoping for some pizza for breakfast.

"No way," I said. "Hot pizza for breakfast? Yuck. It has to cool off, be room temperature before it's edible in the morning."

"Ha," said Brother Malachi. "What you poor souls eat here isn't pizza. Come to Chicago, and I'll show you real pizza, not bread with canned tomato sauce and cheese."

"No way Chicago pizza is better than New York pizza. In New York, you can walk and eat at the same time. Fold it up and enjoy," said Maurice.

They continued debating the merits of pizza styles until we got to the door of the dining hall. I kept out of it, just happy to be with friends.

A Hammer stood guard, making sure our secrets remained that way. Inside the dining hall, the high table was in its customary place, but the other tables had been removed. The room didn't look right anymore—it was hollow, and had the sadness of an empty stadium.

Row upon row of chairs had been set up. They swung around the hall in a U-shape, leaving a twenty-foot square opening in front of the high table. Monks were milling about, some finding places, others trying to make order out of the chaos, and a few helping set up. We were directed to the right side.

"That's not good," said Brother Malachi when we reached our chairs. Each one had a name on it, and we were going to have to sit apart from each other. My chair was in the first row. Rather than sit immediately, we stood talking and watching the final preparations.

"What's not good?' asked Maurice.

"We're sitting to the left of the high table. The left hand side, symbolically, is the side of the criminals. Or the ones who have to prove something. The bishop is already indicating we're guilty." He frowned a bit and shook his head. He rubbed his forehead with one hand and then said, "We have to prove otherwise."

The hall filled up quickly. An iPod and speakers were brought in and placed on a corner of the high table. Large packets of papers were arranged before each chair. Brothers Scott, Robert, and Walter—the Hammers who'd rescued me from the hospital and led the unsanctioned mission—were in our section, along with a few other Hammers I didn't know. Some of the Venerated, retired Inquisitors, were also there.

Brother Otto came in.

I went to him, away from the others.

He gave me a weak smile and asked how I was doing.

"I'm fine, I guess. Brother, look, I know when you sent me to Providence, you thought it was going to be easy, and it went sideways. But I don't blame you for what happened. There was no way you could've known."

He gave me a sad look. "Thank you for that, but it may be a while before I can forgive myself. After this is over, we'll discuss what to do next, but I'm not sure I can teach you anymore." He walked off, leaving me with my mouth hanging open.

He didn't want to teach me anymore. He was rejecting me. I hadn't been made a full Inquisitor, finished up all my final requirements. I'd have to go back to being an apprentice. I'd have to wait for some other Inquisitor to take me on, and who'd do that now with all this controversy?

I walked back to my chair in a daze and flopped down. More people filtered in and took their seats. Someone walked up to our group and addressed us, but I didn't pay any attention until someone gave me a sharp poke with their elbow.

I looked up, and Brother Geoffrey was standing in front of us. He had impatience written all over his frowning face.

"Yes, Brother?" I asked.

"I said I've been assigned as your legate, like a lawyer, which I used to be, God forgive me. I asked if you wanted to describe what occurred on this series of missions. My recommendation is not to do so. They already have your debriefs. If you forget something or leave it out, you'll look like you're hiding something. Like you're guilty."

"No. I've told my story plenty of times," I said.

"Very well. They'll play the debrief or read a transcript of what you said to everyone for the official record. If they leave anything out, let me know. If any questions are asked, answer them briefly and to the point." He leaning forward, staring intently into my eyes. "Keep your comments short. Long winded answers appear to be evasions."

I nodded in understanding and went back to my own private misery. My dark voice mocked and ridiculed me, and I didn't have the strength to fight it.

I was elbowed again, and I turned to see Brother Paul sitting next to me. He'd been a doctor before this life and had helped patch me up in the hospital. "Snap out of it," he said. "If you get all wrapped up in feeling sorry for yourself, you won't be the only one punished. Think of the others, people who risked everything to rescue you and keep you safe. You're letting them down."

That worked. I sat up straighter and knuckled an eye socket to shut up the darkness. When I turned around in my chair, the faces on my side of the room looked worried, except Brother Malachi, who was inspecting his fingernails. Thomas was slumped on the other side, his face drawn and one fist clenched. I gave him a small wave, but he didn't seem to notice.

A little podium was brought out and set up in the middle of the open space, facing the high table. The monks stopped talking quietly amongst themselves. A few minutes later, the door behind the high table opened, and the dignitaries came out. Brother Fred, the head of our order, led the way. I had to stop myself from gaping. When I last saw him, months ago, we'd all completed a run and, despite the limp, he'd finished well. He was a fit fifty or so then, but now his face was pale, his brow furrowed, and his shoulders hunched. He looked old and tired. Behind him, Brother John had an angry look on his face—always a dangerous sign. Next was Bishop Bathoie. His face was reddish and his mouth compressed in a tight line. He walked stiffly, his arms barely moving. The next two I didn't recognize, probably secretaries or aides, and then last was Cardinal Rodgers. I'd never seen the cardinal before, but the red robes gave him away. They lined up behind their seats, except for one of the assistants, who walked over to a small lectern off to one side.

"Let us pray," he said.

We all dutifully stood and bowed our heads. The secretary read off a small prayer, asking for God's guidance and help. When the prayer was over, we sat back down. The cardinal sat in the middle high-backed chair, with Brother Fred on one side and Bishop Bathoie on the other. The secretary remained where he was and continued

"Brethren, we are gathered here today to find the truth of what happened to Apprentice Sebastian these last few days, and what caused him and Brother Captain Walter to launch an unauthorized mission, steal Church property, and cause the death of many Inquisitors, active and retired. Further, once the facts are presented, we will determine what punishment shall be appropriate for them as well as their accomplices. I declare this Court of Inquiry now open."

CHAPTER 10

The cardinal, who'd been reading from a stack of papers, looked up and nodded once the noise died down. I was called up first.

I slowly walked up to the little podium, Brother Geoffrey right behind me.

When I got there, a monk from the other side of the room rose. "Brother Sebastian, would you like to tell us the events that led you to perform an unauthorized mission?"

So it's going to be like that, is it?

The secretary had already referred to me as an apprentice instead of Inquisitor-in-training, demoting me. Now they were going to try to lay all the blame at my feet.

I took a deep, calming breath and gathered my thoughts. "My debrief with Brother Mike is complete and accurate."

A sour look appeared on his face. "You deny stealing Church property to carry out a private vendetta, getting fourteen monks killed in the process?"

Before I could answer, Brother Geoffrey spoke to the high table. "Your Excellency, if we could have the recording of Brother Sebastian's debrief played, that might answer Brother Jim's questions and save everyone time."

Cardinal Rodgers nodded his assent, and a few seconds later, my recorded voice filled the room. There were occasional murmurs from the crowd, and I tried very hard to remain impassive during the difficult parts. The memories were still painful, and hearing my own words, being the center of attention like this, hurt.

When it was over, there was silence. Brother Geoffrey was the first to speak. "Does Your Excellency have any questions?"

Cardinal Rodgers didn't even look at me. "No."

The rest of the trial seemed to go quickly. Brother Malachi stood up even before I got to my seat and marched to the podium. His debrief was played for all to hear. He talked about how he'd learned of the bone needle from Brother Paul, and had instructed the Hammers to prepare an ambush for Thaddeus and get me out of the Rectory. Brother Malachi had also told everyone to keep me in the dark until the bone needle was removed. He went on to say he'd called Bishop Bathoie's secretary to tell him what was happening, to keep him apprised of events. Heads turned at this, and the secretary who'd read the introduction shrank a little and nodded at the wordless question.

When it was over, the cardinal had no questions for him. He did give a long look to Bishop Bathoie. The bishop's face turned red, but his gaze remained fixed straight ahead. Brother Walter was next, and his debrief parroted Brother Malachi's.

Brother Paul's debrief talked about the hospital and what had occurred there, our escape to a nearby Rectory, the bone needle, and Brother Malachi's instructions. On and on it went, each person's debrief matching what Brother Malachi had said. Bishop Bathoie continued to stare straight ahead, and his face was turning from red to purple with suppressed rage.

The first surprise was Maurice's debrief. He'd come to visit me when I was in the hospital. I was a bit of a mess, and he'd helped cheer me up. I didn't know it at the time, but he was still in the hospital when the witches came to kill me. He managed to Purge a witch and an ogre himself. There were a few murmurs at this from the other monks, and when he came back to our section, he had a cocky grin on his face. I couldn't help but smile at little. He must've been bursting to tell me, but held off to help me get through my own troubles. I gave him a thumbs up and a nod.

Things are going well.

My final surprise was when Brother Otto was called. Like everyone else, he asked for his debrief to be played, and hung his head as though praying. His debrief focused a lot on me. How he was concerned about my adjustment as an Inquisitor, how he'd held me back over my obsession with tracking down the witch who'd killed my family. He talked about his feelings of failure in my instruction, and how he didn't believe he would be able to instruct me anymore. He ended with an apology to me and to the Brethren for failing us.

There was a long silence after the recording stopped.

He'd sold me out. I'd been in the clear, but by disavowing me, Brother Otto had painted me as a semi-crazy loose cannon. I could feel the eyes on me; some would wonder for a moment, others just accept. There was no way to recover from that. No one else would take a chance on instructing me. From hero to liability in ten minutes.

Cardinal Rodgers, looking at Brother Otto, asked his first question. "Brother, are you asking to be relieved of your duty?"

Head still low, Brother Otto said, "Yes, Your Excellency."

The cardinal looked perplexed. His eyes flitted from Brother Otto to me and then back to him again. "But why?"

The question lingered, and everyone was silent, waiting for the answer. It was slow in coming, and the worst cut yet.

"I'm not strong enough to keep him in check. I fear for his safety and mine."

I felt gutted. Worthless. Everything I'd done up to this point was in vain; my success, gone. Maybe what he'd said was true. Maybe I'd let down a friend, a mentor. Brother Otto had trained me since I was an apprentice. He'd coached me through the difficult times, taught me how to be a better man and Inquisitor. He went with me to visit my wife's grave, even though I was still wanted by the police. He was the one who'd procured my wedding photo, and now…now he was abandoning me. I wanted to sink down into the floor and never get up again.

A sharp elbow dug into my side, and Brother Paul leaned into me. "Keep your head up. Don't let them win. If you're willing to carry bandages, I'll take you as my apprentice."

I'd like to say I was grateful, but I was too busy feeling like a dog turd to thank him. I did sit up a bit though.

Brother Otto didn't even look at me when he returned to his seat.

The cardinal, having reached some decision after listening to our debriefs, stood up. "Unless there are any more facts to be presented…" He scanned the room, which remained silent. "I see no reason to admonish anyone for this mission, even if it ended tragically. It's well within a Plenipotentiary's authority to set up a mission, and to compel others to assist. Brother Malachi did try to keep the bishop informed of events, and Brother Walter and the others were following orders. Brother Sebastian bears no responsibility for participating in the mission as he was unaware of it not being approved, and was under the command of Brother Malachi in any event. I declare this Inquest over."

Monks rose, talking excitedly. The cardinal had already turned to leave the dining hall when a loud voice rang out, "Everyone remain where you are!" It was Bishop Bathoie. He turned and walked to the cardinal. They had a brief, and—it looked to me—heated discussion a few paces away from the others.

Finally, the cardinal shook his head and walked away, with one of the secretaries following.

Now things get nasty.

"Sit!" commanded the bishop. He gave us a long glare, anger radiating from him. "I'm pleased that the results of the Inquest were so favorable," he said, but his rigid body posture and snarl gave away his true feelings. "Even so, I believe some changes need to be made." He looked over the hall, his gaze coming to rest on our section. "Brother Walter, you are released from all duties here in New England. I ask you and your team to leave for your monastery now. Neither you nor any member of your team will be welcome here for a period of five years. It is my hope that you will learn humility during that time. If you return," he said, the emphasis leaving no doubt that Walter was banished for life, "perhaps you will have learned to adopt a more deferential attitude."

Brother Walter and the other Hammers stood, and, like a military unit, turned as one and marched out. Eyes followed their progress. No one objected; no one made a sound. Their footsteps were loud and the door made a small boom when it closed behind them.

Bishop Bathoie just stood there, staring at their progress and seeming smaller for the pettiness of his actions. When the door closed, he turned back looking where I and the others sat. "Brother Malachi, I can't remove you from New England, but be assured, while I am bishop, you will not be welcome."

I turned, expecting Brother Malachi to get up and cuss the bishop out or flip him off or something. Unrealistic, of course, but I expected defiance. He just sat there, his face and posture placid. He gave a small nod.

When I turned back, the bishop was looking directly at me. "Brother Sebastian," he said. "You will revert to apprentice status, and, as no one will train you—"

Several Inquisitors stood.

"I'll train him," said one monk I'd never laid eyes on before.

"I will come out of retirement to train the boy," said Brother Giuseppe. Heads turned at that.

My spirits soared. I wasn't damaged goods; I could get fully trained, and move on.

The bishop looked back and forth at the standing Inquisitors and me, clearly shocked at this show of support. "No," he said. "Brother Sebastian will not be staying here. He will be transferred to our monastery in Missouri, where he can be trained properly."

"That's a very poor decision, Your Holiness," said Brother Giuseppe.

There was a collective intake of breath, and monks who'd been observing Brother Giuseppe's outburst whipped around to see the bishop's reaction.

Surprisingly, the bishop's face softened, and he smiled a little. "Perhaps you are right, Brother," he said. "But you have chosen your path, and I have chosen mine. It is my decision, and I make it thus." He looked back at me. "Go pack your things, Apprentice."

I had been rejected. Rejected and sent away like a dog that couldn't be housebroken. Instead of crawling under my chair and hiding, I stood with all the dignity I could muster. My head held high, I walked out, looking at no one, acknowledging nothing. It was a lie. My dark voice laughed and taunted the whole way.

The door loomed in front of me and then I was outside. The door closed behind me automatically and with finality. My pace was slow across the grounds to the Inquisitors' Residence, my feet dragging and my eyes suddenly blurry.

After packing what few things I owned, I sat on my bed, waiting for someone to collect me. There was no blubbering, but I did have to wipe my eyes frequently. I was being cast out, and it burned and knotted me up inside.

CHAPTER 11

A long time later, there was a knock at my door, and Brother Malachi came in with a few bags, a case, and a black eye.

"What happened?" I asked, my misery forgotten for a moment.

"I had a disagreement with Brother Rodger, but we worked it out in the end."

"What happened?" I repeated.

"I thought you might want your backpack and some gear. Brother John gave me the bag easily enough, but Brother Rodger was unwilling to let you have your MP-5 and pistol. He was under the belief that since you're going to another monastery, you should be equipped there. I disagreed."

"My backpack?" I said, reaching for it. Fear and hope warred within me. I knelt down and opened the back pocket. It was still there, my wife and I smiling for the camera in front of the altar.

"Brother John kept your secret safe from the bishop."

I couldn't look away from Sarah's smiling face. Brother Otto had gotten me the picture, a memory of a life I longed to return to, but couldn't.

And what does Brother Otto think of you now? The dark voice in my head laughed.

"Why...why did Brother Otto—" My eyes filled again, and I put the picture away before I damaged it.

"I don't know. I didn't ask him, and he probably can't give a good reason. Maybe it's jealousy. Maybe the bishop got to him. Maybe you're just too good."

"Huh?" I said, looking up at him.

"I still think Otto's a good man, a good monk. I think his decision was poorly made, and it'll bother him for a long time. Perhaps, in his mind, you're more than he can handle. You've advanced too far. You've moved too fast. There has to be a level of respect between teacher and instructor, and maybe now he sees you as an equal. Maybe he isn't sure you're ready, because he can't judge an equal."

They were just words to me. I was still being sent away. Still a disappointment to those I admired and trusted. My navel gazing and self-loathing were interrupted by Brother Malachi saying something.

"Could you repeat that, Brother?"

"I said it is really for the best, you being sent away."

"Excuse me?" Anger welled up inside me. I clenched my fists and shouted, "It's good to be publicly shamed like that, to be sent away, and have to qualify all over again, if I can ever get anyone to instruct me?"

His eyes went cold, his face hard and dangerous. "Do not yell at me, Apprentice. Calm yourself and listen."

His words washed over me, but the expression stopped me cold. It gave me a moment to realize what he'd said. "Apprentice?" I asked tentatively.

"Yes, idiot, I'm going to instruct you."

Humility and hope and gratitude all flooded into me at once. I managed to choke out, "Thank you."

His face softened a bit. "Be careful thanking me. You won't be so happy once we leave here, and there are two more matters to clear up." He held up a finger. "First, you're not good enough to be my apprentice. You need more training. We'll stop at Missouri, and then we're off to Arizona. Once you complete the Hammer course, we can begin training. Only then will you be ready to keep up with me."

"How long?" I asked.

"Normally, it takes a couple of years, but that's starting at a novice level. I figure for you, somewhere between fifteen and eighteen months. It's hard, and you'll hate me often for sending you there. In the end, though, it will be worth it, for you and for me. When you finish, no one will ever be able to question your ability to be an Inquisitor."

I just nodded.

It's not like you have any other choices, whispered the dark voice, but I was too happy to pay attention to it.

"I had a long talk with Brother Paul. He consulted with some other doctors, and they decided the best way for you to regain your ability to hear pitch is for you to learn to play an instrument." He pointed to a long flat case in the pile. "Since you seem to like the violin, I've gotten you one, along with an electronic tuner and metronome. You'll use the tuner to see if a note's in tune, even if you can't hear it. Even if your brain isn't sure, the tuner won't lie, and your fingers will eventually figure out where to go. It'll take you a long time to regain your ability to understand music, so every night you are to try to play for at least thirty minutes. We'll see about some instruction. I was a trumpet man, myself."

It was too much. I didn't know what to say or do. I just sat there, mouth flapping.

Brother Malachi saved me again. "Let's go. We have a long trip ahead of us." We picked up the gear and headed out.

CHAPTER 12

Sebastian
Now

When we got to Arizona, it took one conversation and thirty minutes, and I was in the next class of Hammers. Brother Malachi drove off that afternoon after wishing me luck. I thought I was ready. I wasn't.

I will not fail became my mantra.

I endured. In some ways, it was enough. Most of the time it was all I had—my determination to keep going, to prove to those who doubted me that I was good enough to be one of the Brethren, to be called Inquisitor.

We learned what it took to be a Hammer. Hammers hunt the most dangerous kind of witches: Screwfaces. Even with their training, weapons, and blitz attacks, Hammers still died in droves on a Purge. Screwfaces are the enforcers of the witch community. More vicious than a maddened badger, they delight in pain, both given and received. Their most terrible power is the ability to keep a victim alive. Alive, despite having every inch of skin burned off. Alive, despite being impaled from anus to torso. Despite blood loss, injury, or even putrefaction. Alive for weeks, until madness set in.

They showed us pictures and had us read accounts of past missions and the atrocities committed by Screwfaces. Hammers came in and lectured us. It was the best they could do to prep us, but even then it wasn't the same as actually being there. Some, when they went on an actual mission and saw the results of a Screwface's torture, had gone catatonic. Become shells of their former selves, bodies with no minds, waiting to die. Perhaps I was lucky, in some twisted way. I'd had my baptism of horror in that baleful town of Providence, and even though it haunted me still, I'd survived.

The fifteen months I'd spent learning to be a Hammer were mostly a blur, like a half remembered nightmare of pain, discomfort, and dread. Half our class had failed one portion or another and had to repeat. Several were injured and couldn't continue, a few even died. Their memorials were short and hurried, almost as though the Hammers were embarrassed.

I would've walked away a dozen times, but I had nowhere else to go. I had no family anymore—their murder was my introduction into this realm of madness. There was no one to shelter me and nowhere to hide. I was still wanted by the police, witches would hunt me down and kill me before I could expose or kill them, and the bishop had banished me. Only Brother Malachi had faith in me, and I wasn't going to let him down. I had something to prove, to myself and everyone in the Brethren, so I got up every time I was knocked down and worked through the pain and cold and terror.

I never gave up, and now, finally, I was almost done.

I looked up, past the dusty brown rock of Zola Butte worn smooth by wind and rain, with not a handhold in sight. Twenty more feet to the top of the cliff, but it might as well have been a million miles. Squinting in the bright light and dust, I searched in vain for a way up the rock. My arms were already starting to quiver. I had to move, and soon, but I was so tired.

I will not fail.

My left arm was shaking from the strain. If I didn't get moving soon, I'd fall. I was so tired, I had to refocus on what I was doing and why.

I squinted and shifted my grip a bit, taking stock of my situation.

You're up a cliff doing what hospitals call "organ donation." You have no ropes or safety gear. A freestyle climb for those who like to laugh at death. You have at least twenty more feet to go, and you're out of handholds.

A depressing but accurate summation.

74

I was stuck and going to have to make a hallelujah leap. There was a narrow crack off to my left, some weakness where the rock had been worn away by water and time. It started just below me and ran up to the top. It looked like it might hold me, but I wouldn't know until it was too late.

"I will not fail," I reminded myself and let go of the solid grip I had with my right hand. I could feel myself starting to fall away from the rock face as I moved, but I couldn't stop now. Once the fingertips of my right hand were set, I moved my left hand to the crack while making a fist. I wedged it in as an anchor. Releasing my right hand, I started to swing free. I bicycled my legs to keep from wrenching my left arm out of the socket or losing the grip, and pulled myself up with one arm until I could use my other hand.

Once my right fist was solidly wedged, I relaxed my left hand. I'd anticipated the pain, but it still made me shiver. Slowly, I eased my way up, first leaving skin and then blood. My progress seemed to be measured in inches, and after every move up, I had to rest for a minute. About the time my arms were almost useless with fatigue, the crack widened and I could use my legs. My progress would've been faster, but the last three days of my final practical had exhausted me. Eventually, I made it to the top and was able to drag myself over.

They were waiting there for me—the Brothers Grimm, as I called them, but only in my head. Brother Jim, Brother Rex, and Brother Tomas. I was almost done; as soon as I could stand up and give my report, it would all be over.

I lay there on the top of the butte for a minute, chest heaving and arms burning from the strain, gathering my strength. The wind moved hot air around, coating me with a fine layer of dust, but I was past caring about things like cleanliness. I quivered and twitched, physically spent. I felt the Brothers Grimm staring disapprovingly at my weakness, their eyes burning holes into my back.

I will not fail. I pushed myself up and staggered over to them.

"Brother Sebastian reports," I said, pulling my notebook out of a pocket.

"Brother Sebastian reports what?" said Brother Jim. I couldn't tell if he disliked me personally or just saw me as a liability until I'd proven myself.

I read my report right there, baking in the sun.

When I was finished, the monks glanced at each other and nodded in silent approval. Brother Jim turned back to me and said, "Acceptable. Eat this," he pulled a candy bar from a pouch, "and you may sleep for four hours." He waved a hand toward a cot under some trees.

"Acceptable" was high praise from him. Usually I received a long lecture on the many mistakes I'd made, followed by some physical activity, like running, as penance. I took the candy bar and wolfed it down in three bites. I stuffed the wrapper in a pocket as I walked slowly over to the cot and gratefully sank down, quickly falling into a deep sleep.

I dreamed, my brain punishing me for some sin or another. It started with a view of my wife, naked and pregnant, sitting in a chair.

"Hand me my cello, honey. I want to play you some music."

I looked around, but there was nothing but her and me and the chair she sat in. "I can't find it," I stammered.

"Don't you love me?" she said, and blood oozed from her mouth.

I tried to move, but my feet were missing. Somehow I'd merged with the floor from the ankles down.

"Why don't you love me?" she asked, and with a sick *thock*, an invisible blow struck her chest. Ribs broke and sprayed an impossible amount of blood over us both. "Why don't you love me?" she asked again as another blow landed and her face was split open. Her eyes, her beautiful eyes, never blinked, never left my face, pinned me in place like a bug in a specimen tray. I wailed, and I cried, but I couldn't move. I couldn't stop staring into her questioning eyes.

Blood pooled at the ends of my legs and rose quickly.

"Why don't you love me?" she asked me again and again.

The blood rose until I drowned.

CHAPTER 13

I woke when I hit the ground face-first. I struggled to get up, almost swimming in the dry desert dust. The cot was on top of me. A glance up showed me Brother Tomas standing over me.

"Wake up," said Brother Tomas, the least scary of the Brothers Grimm. "You've been asleep an hour. It's now nine o'clock."

After wiping the tears from my face, spitting out sand, and disentangling myself, I managed to stand. My legs wobbled a bit, my mind still dealing with the dream. I took a few deep breaths to calm down, which I masked by appearing to stretch, then turned back to Brother Tomas. A hard life had left him looking older than he was, and his face—scarred and weather-beaten—would never be called handsome. His dirty blond hair tended to curl and would've been feminine on a softer, less formidable face. His features were all harsh, but his throat was the object of stares. Like a demented spider web, crisscrossing scars extended from one side to the other. It was obvious there'd been repeated trauma and from different sources. Some of the scars were more recent—red and angry-looking—while others looked more like bites or punctures. Normally Brother Tomas kept his shirt buttoned to his chin to spare the rest of us, but today, in the desert heat, he'd relented. Even after all this time, I still found it hard not to stare.

"Sorry," I said, "bad dream."

Brother Tomas almost looked concerned, his brown eyes searching. It was, for just a moment, as though he cared. It only lasted a heartbeat. The expression was gone in a flash, and the mask of hardness returned. "We can talk about it later if you need to do so. Put that behind you and prepare. There's been a problem."

He gave no further explanation, which was something I'd come to expect here. An instructor would make a statement, and the student was expected to divine all possible meanings and responses required. Then the student had to either give the correct response or ask the question that would elicit the most information.

With a deep breath, I shook my head to get back into the present. I'd weep later. "How can I help?" It was the only acceptable response I could give. I hoped it was the reply he was looking for—I had no desire for a lecture or calisthenics so I could focus my mind, having not realized the proper answer was "forty-two dolphins."

He gave a short nod and seemed almost pleased. I mentally let out a sigh of relief as he began talking. "We have witch movement in our area," he said. "There've been sightings and reports coming in from all over the state and nearby areas, giving us advance warning."

Weird.

Witches, as a rule, kept away from each other. They set up their little fiefdoms of insanity and guarded them well. A witch on the move was one in trouble, running from a defeat. If this wasn't the case then there was another reason, one I didn't know about. I liked mysteries, but to discover them myself, not be lectured as though I were a dim pupil.

I waited for more, but he continued staring at me. The wind swirled, scattering dust in little tornados. I could just make out the other two Brothers animatedly talking with each other.

"Are they moving through the area or congregating?" I asked.

I was rewarded with another small nod, indicating I'd asked the correct question. I'd found this method of training infuriating at first, but eventually got used to it. The slow pace made me think, and it also definitely cut down on the questions and chatter. "That's all we have at the moment. We're trying to get more information before we decide whether to move or warn others."

That was an unexpected response. I'd been taught that the Hammers didn't "warn others;" they fought.

What's the point of all this...this pain and blood and misery if we've merely become scouts? There has to be more.

I sorted through possible questions until I hit on one that could answer my many questions at once. "How many witches are we talking about?"

"We have reliable sightings of five independent groups so far," he said.

"Groups?" I blurted, my dread increasing. I'd never heard of a witch moving her entire retinue from one place to another over a long distance. Witches fled when they lost a fight, if they could, but that was her and maybe a minion she hadn't sacrificed to escape, not a group. A witch mobilizing for a threat might move herself and her minions, but that was for a short duration and over a short distance, not across counties and state lines.

"Yes," said Brother Thomas, "these appear to be full-scale migrations." He paused for a moment to let this sink in. "There are at least three sightings that include multiple minions. They're marching to war." He tilted his head to one side a bit as though thinking. "Why the mass mobilizations?" he asked rhetorically. "We don't know, but we need to find out and stop it before they can do whatever it is they're attempting, or the locals get trampled in the fighting."

"Five is a lot for one area," I said, keeping the concern out of my voice, stalling for time.

It wasn't a good answer, but my head was swirling with possibilities and questions. Five groups was an impossible number as far as I was concerned. I'd never heard of something like this, even in our history classes.

"The witches we can spot are easy," said Brother Thomas, "the real danger is the ones hidden."

"You think there are more?"

Brother Thomas paused at this, and his expression turned softer. "I worry about two things: what I don't know and what I don't understand." He paused for a beat. "I spend a lot of my time worrying."

I think it was supposed to be a joke, but it seemed far too paranoid to be funny to me.

"What we're going to do," he continued, "is return to the priory and prepare."

We broke down the camp, made our way down the mesa, loaded up the waiting SUV, and drove away. On the road, the Brothers Grimm said little. I sat in the back, alone with my uncertainty.

CHAPTER 14

James

Yun Cho was, at first glance, prey. She was deceptively small, almost childlike in build, but her appearance was a lie. With the magi, size usually equates to power, but not in her case. The strength and fury contained in her four-foot-eleven body had fooled and then eliminated quite a few. It would've been easy to think of her as weak, someone to toy with before destroying. I wasn't deceived.

When I met her, she was already part of Thaddeus's coven. She was stronger and knew more of the mysteries of the magi than I. Thaddeus instructed her to teach me, and her lessons were brutal things, filled with pain and torment. Her mastery of a pain lance, a fun little spell that sets nerve endings on fire, was revealed to me time and again. Even when not engaged in lessons, she humiliated me, as the strong will do to the weak. I took it as stoically as I could, biding my time for a chance at revenge. Now, with one look, I knew who the master was.

Her hair, long and dark and always a mess, seemed even more unkempt and wild. Her eyes had a feral gleam, and she smiled in a way that would've been most at home in an insane asylum. Before going into full death-to-the-world bloodlust, she had the unfortunate habit of giggling—not a giggle of happiness, but the titter of a serial killer with her latest victim, knowing the agony, and blood, and screams would last for days. We both knew she'd lose if we fought, but showing weakness was death in the magi world. There were appearances to maintain. She had to bluster, convince me she was too much of a threat to fight. I had to remain unconcerned by her displays. It was a tiresome dance, but to ignore it would invite attack, and I had places to be.

I'd stopped the car at an intersection to check directions when she appeared. I was fully in the desert now, and the two-lane road vanished off into the horizon. The occasional sign was holed by the mindless cattle shooting at it for fun or in a drunken desire to destroy things. A wavering barbed wire fence undercut by dry washes and gullies kept in the clumps of cacti. Farther off were mesas and hills. I'd been about to turn right on Rural Route 17, another deserted road, to head north when she popped up from a small gully near the road and attacked. She'd let loose with a ring of flame, which surrounded the car. The flames blazed up high then dropped down to a few feet. It was meant to overawe me and freeze me in place. Impressive for conies, but a bit low level for me. Three werewolves were arrayed behind her. Through the flames, we locked eyes and recognized each other at once. I raised one eyebrow in an amused sort of way.

"James," she said as fire roiled around one hand, "what brings you out here?"

The flames around the car were already dying off. I got out of the car slowly, with a studied nonchalance. Driving off would've been a sign of weakness.

Anyway, perhaps she has some information I can use.

My MP-5 was dragged along by the sling. A light smack on my leg let me know it was there and ready if I needed it. I didn't glance at it or lay a hand on it, but one of the werewolves moved toward me. Werewolves were low-level transmutations—stupid, and hard to control. They were something a new witch might create, believing they would keep her safe. The smarter ones used them as cannon fodder, or a distraction from the real threat. The Yun I knew wouldn't have bothered with such simplistic brutes. Something had changed, and not for the better.

Yun raised her non-ensorcelled hand quickly to check the werewolf's movement toward me. Like a well-trained dog, it froze. I flicked dust off my vest and didn't look back into Yun's eyes. I kept my face neutral, not showing my rage.

"If you needed a ride, you could've just asked," I said blandly, "or gotten a coney to do it."

She paused, and the fire in her hand winked out. "I heard the scream," she said, "and have come to my master's call."

I almost laughed. Yun had escaped from Thaddeus before I led the revolt. She hadn't been enthralled as she was one of Thaddeus's favorites, as was I, and he was grooming her to be something more than a simple drudge. She figured out how to slip past the wards and disappeared one night. It was a blow to Thaddeus, as he'd believed that she, like all his followers and minions, was happy, not realizing or caring that she might've had ambitions of her own.

Thaddeus had seen her departure as a betrayal and had several temper tantrums over it, destroying things and lashing out at others. Her absence and his lack of focus had weakened him enough for the coup to succeed, and her return to him now was suspicious. My mind raced furiously, trying to understand the situation before I made a decision. It was one of the things that had slowed my growth as a magi, but paid off in the end as I didn't make foolish mistakes, like some. Why would Yun want to serve Thaddeus again?

She's weak, I thought with an internal smile. She needed his protection, as impossible as that was—he was unlikely to be in a forgiving mood. She had to be desperate, with few, or no, other options.

"And why would you return to Thaddeus?" I asked, though I doubted she'd tell me the truth.

"He made promises, guarantees to me." An obvious lie. Thaddeus might teach, he might inflict pain on a whim, but he did not make promises.

"You mean you want to plunder his mind while he's still weak."

"I was always loyal," she said, whining just a little.

I didn't bother arguing with her over her absurd definition of loyalty. "Good for you. What does that have to do with me?"

"Thaddeus will require your support to hunt down those who tried to banish him."

"I doubt he'll need my help, or even notice my absence."

"Our master requires our help."

"He stopped being my master a while back." It was the wrong thing to say. If I wasn't part of Thaddeus's coven, I was an enemy.

Her eyes opened wide.

I recognized the warning and grabbed my MP-5 with one hand, crouching to make myself a smaller target. At the same time, I reached into my vest and brought out the severed hand. Running would've been preferable, but there was no way to outrun the werewolves. This would have to be settled with pain and blood. With a single thought, there was a snap, and a purple-black flaming halo of magical power materialized from the severed hand I held.

I spoke the words of power, *"Pakkkmav Xervi Fqss,"* to complete one of the spells contained within. The hand vibrated and thrummed with power, summoning Hell serpents. Tubes, a shade of neon red that hurt the eye and faded in and out of reality, leaped forth to do my will. There was no front or back, no head or tail, and no need for such features with these creatures—they existed only to rend flesh and feed. They moved almost faster than the eye could track, speeding across the road and desert before burrowing into the bodies of the werewolves.

The three werewolves stopped mid-bound. The Hell serpents hit flesh and tunneled in and up until they came out of their heads. Black, motor-oil shiny blood, mixed with bits of brain and bone, fountained up. The Hell serpents emerged right behind the spray and back out into the sky. Their feeding complete, they winked out of existence with a twisting of reality. The bodies of the werewolves crumpled into cored heaps. They didn't even have time to whimper.

The two remaining Hell serpents were circling Yun, who'd hastily set up a lesser ring of warding. I could just see the sick green of her power wafting up to the empty sky like heat waves. The Hell serpents couldn't cross the circle, and every time they got too close, the vapors snapped solid. A low moan of frustration came from them as they were denied food. Realization hit me. Yun didn't attack—hadn't saved her werewolves—because she couldn't. She was about out of power or no longer had any spell repositories. Either way, she might as well have been a coney.

Prey, and all mine.

A rare genuine smile formed as I walked over. The Hell serpents continued circling the ward. Given time, they'd leave the area, hunting for food. That might expose me, and I needed to be unobtrusive. For now. I flicked my hand, and they gave a final moan of frustration and rippled away into nothing. All was still. I stood there, reveling in the moment. The sky was a light blue, brownish hills lumped off into the distance, and wind stirred the dust. Yun's eyes were wide and scared—the eyes of a doe the moment before the wolves pounced. Everything seemed just right. I could almost taste her helplessness.

The green vapors slowly rose between us. The circle could stop a minor summoned creature, but not a physical attack. She might as well have been hiding behind a piece of paper. She stared back, looking shocked, the defiance gone from her face as she was reduced to a scared little girl. Two knives, cruelly shaped, were held in shaking hands—her last defense, and worthless against me. I lowered my MP-5. I wouldn't need it.

I shook my head at her pathetic state. "Answer my questions, and I may leave you in peace. Defy me, and I'll compel you to cut off your own head."

Yun held my gaze for a moment as though searching for weakness, or pity, or another chance, and found nothing. She bowed her head and lowered the knives.

A wash of satisfaction, almost orgasmic, went through me as I savored her defeat. I'd missed this life. I'd known, right after I'd killed Thaddeus, that there was no way I could return to the mysteries of the magi. Thaddeus had allies who would seek me out. He had debts that some would expect me to pay. Weaklings looking for protection who would expose me. And, of course, my former Brethren were always looking to Purge the magi. A heretic like myself, someone who'd left them behind and embraced magic, was at the top of their to-do list, as I might tempt others away. Hiding, sinking into the sea of humanity, had been the best way to keep myself safe at the time, but I'd missed out on so much fun. There were no challenges with Olivia; I always knew what to do to keep her in line. She wasn't magi. She couldn't see. She was a pet, limited to a few useful tricks. Life was safe, but dreary. I felt like I'd woken from a deep slumber and was ready to bend the world to my will once again.

"Who did this to you?" I asked.

"Krypkie." I knew who she meant in an instant. He was a necromancer. When Thaddeus led us to Arizona, we'd passed through Krypkie's territory. Foolishly, Krypkie had sent a lich to measure our abilities. Vile, filthy creatures, lichs are really nothing more than intelligent ghouls—the kind of creature you might send after one of the false monks, but not one of the magi. It was insulting. With contemptuous ease, Thaddeus had broken the binding that allowed Krypkie to control the lich then imposed his own will upon it, and learned all about the foolish necromancer. When Thaddeus had his answers, he sent the lich back to hunt its former master. It was a sublime bit of revenge for the insult, but, apparently, Krypkie had survived the reversal.

"How?"

"Krypkie knows, somehow he knows Thaddeus has returned. He's searching for Thaddeus's location, and when he spotted me, he tried to trap me. He has a re-animation."

"What?" I said. Re-animations are what Mary Shelley wrote about: a mass of lifeless tissue brought back. Different from clockworks or golems, which were never alive, once brought back, the re-animation could "think," in a limited fashion. Supposedly incredibly hard and complex to create, having one is the sign of a master necromancer. Something had changed. Krypkie had gotten much better, stronger, than when he'd sent his pitiful scout to spy on us.

"He has a re-animation," she cried again. "It killed my thrall, Shelia, and all my pets. I fled with the dogs Shelia made yesterday. I used the last of my power to bind them to me and haven't been able to find a coney to replenish it."

I pondered her situation for a moment. There was more, and I doubted she was without *any* power. None of us were that stupid.

She'd encountered Krypkie, he'd overpowered her, and she'd fled, abandoning everything to make sure she got clear. Nothing abnormal there. No, the real issue was that Krypkie knew about Thaddeus's return. That was a problem.

What does Krypkie know? How does he know? Are there others?

I answered my own question: *If Krypkie knows, there will be others.*

I'd have to be even more cautious on my return to the house. I shook my head to focus on the immediate problem: Yun. What was I going to do with her? I'd gotten as much useful information as I was going to get. As time passed, she'd get braver, and her answers would be less trustworthy.

Time to end this.

I had no need of a slave, no desire for a partner. Sacrificing her would be fun but time consuming. Still, it didn't seem right to just let her run free. If I didn't teach her proper reverence for her betters, who would?

Looking about for a minute, I spied a small rock by the side of the road. It gave me an idea that I turned over for a few seconds before concluding that it would be the right blend of humiliation, pain, and possible death. Perfect. I retrieved the rock and went back to Yun, who was alternating between scared and hopeful.

"Here's a test for you," I said. "After failing so miserably at handling Krypkie, maybe you can redeem yourself." I set the rock down, and willed power into the hand.

Speaking the words of power hurt. My ears popped, and a tooth felt loose by the time I was done. The rock glowed with the purple-black of true magic. It twisted and grew, transforming into a shape. The head, misshapen with pointy ears and slits for eyes, emerged first, as though being born. The arms, unnaturally long and ending in stubby claws, were next then finally the rest slid free. A squat stone gargoyle, maybe two feet tall, knelt at my feet.

"Master," it said, and its tone was properly reverential, despite the protruding fangs.

I pointed at Yun. "Guard," I commanded the gargoyle. Grinding and cracking, it turned to face her and sat down cross-legged, a few feet away from her silly little circle. The gargoyle couldn't cross the ward, but Yun couldn't leave the circle without being attacked. Normally, Yun could've handled a platoon of these creatures, but powerless as she claimed she was now, all she could do was wait until the situation changed. It was insulting, something one might do to a scrub or even a coney. I felt another smile form as I walked away, ignoring Yun's screams and curses.

CHAPTER 15

Sebastian

On the way back to the priory from Zola Butte, we stopped to pick up another student, Brother Greg.

Dirt encrusted his face and arms, and the faint odor of rotten milk wafted in with him.

"Brothers," he said by way of greeting as he climbed inside, dropping a small folding shovel on the floor at his feet.

We'd never been on the same team in training, but we'd still gravitated toward each other as we were older than most of the others. For a monk about to become one of the super serious Hammers, Brother Greg was pretty normal. He had bright yellow-red hair that he kept in a flat top, freckles, and a propensity to drink and fight. In an unusual moment when we were both so tired we were a bit loopy, he admitted to me that he didn't really like drinking, but "if I'm gonna look Irish, I'm gonna be Irish."

I'd given him a raised fist. "Live the stereotype."

The SUV lurched back onto the road. The Brothers Grimm ignored us—one driving, one talking on the phone, and one staring out the window. Despite the noise of the vehicle and the phone conversation, it seemed oppressively quiet. We were waiting for something, and anticipation congealed the air.

"What's going on?" Brother Greg finally asked.

I glanced around to see if I was supposed to be quiet, but we were being ignored, so I told him what I knew. "Not really sure. Apparently there are some witches moving about. No one knows why or where they're going."

Brother Greg nodded, seemingly unconcerned. "Did you finish?"

I figured he was talking about our final practical. "Yeah, I finished up a bit early. They actually let me take a nap."

"Nice. I'd just finished when you picked me up."

"You were by yourself?" I said. "No proctors waiting for you?"

He shook his head. "Not that I could see. My last task was to dig a hole, bury something, fill it back in, and wait for retrieval. I'd just smoothed out the dirt, covered the area with some rocks and leaves when you arrived."

His final seemed absurdly easy compared to mine.

"Not a body, I hope," I said, trying for humor, something to take my mind off my worry and anger. I had to work at it.

Brother Greg helped. "Don't think so, but it could've been a head, or a squishy bowling ball."

"Did you sanctify the ground first? Hate for it to come back to life. It could use its tongue to drag itself along, looking for revenge."

Brother Greg put on a look of mock horror. "Oh dear me. I completely forgot. What if it gets hold of bat wings and can now fly? What will the world do?"

I started to laugh, something I didn't do very often anymore.

At that moment, Brother Jim, who'd been ignoring us, slapped a hand down. He slowly turned away from the window until he was facing us. His brown eyes darted back and forth between ours and his look was chilly.

I felt myself scrunching down under his stare.

He held that stare for a long minute, making his point. Finally, with a small snort, he turned back to look out the window again.

Brother Greg and I spent the rest of the ride in silence.

The priory was a hive of activity. Monks darted about carrying papers, weapons, and combat gear. Worried faces rushed past us, not even stopping to greet us or acknowledge our return. I could feel the tension in the air the moment we stepped out of the vehicle. None of the Brothers Grimm instructed us to get cleaned up or prepare for our mission debrief. They were silent as they moved off to the chapter house, Brother Greg and I trailing along, exchanging glances and shrugs. I looked around, taking it all in. It might be the last time I ever saw this place. I didn't think I'd miss it.

I bumped into Brother Greg, shaking me out of my thoughts. We weren't headed back to our barracks, but to the main house. I followed our group into the briefing room. Greg didn't even have a chance to get rid of the shovel.

Like all things at the Arizona monastery, the briefing room was bigger and nicer than the one in New England. The center, where the briefer would stand, was sunken. I'd been there myself on two different occasions to brief missions. Once my plans and proposed actions were torn to shreds by the proctors. The second time I got a grunt of acceptance that I counted as a victory. A screen took up one wall of the briefing room. The important people sat at a table on a raised section opposite the screen. At the head of the table was the Master Hammer, with his two deputies on either side. Brother Greg had once told me he thought they should be called Thought and Memory. Not as good as some of Brother Rubin's old puns, back when we were apprentices, but it had made a dreary day a bit better.

The students were clustered together in folding chairs. There was a lot less chatter and good-natured banter with the Hammers than when I was an apprentice. The intensity the Hammers needed seemed to come at the cost of camaraderie and enjoyment of life. They acted more like they were surviving, not living. Their jobs were impossibly hard—many died or were broken—but to me, the worst was the loss of humor and good will. Life was too harsh to give up on levity. What was the point of a dull, gray existence? I missed the banter and jokes and needed them more than ever, but all I got was criticism and more training.

The rest of the room was taken up by actual Hammers as they filtered in. It quieted down quickly as the Master Hammer rose.

"Brothers, it's come to our attention we have witch movement in our area. Brother Sam will present what is known and answer questions as best as he can. It's still early so there will be much we haven't learned yet. We've sent out some scouts. Their reports, along with the ones we've already received, should give us clarity, but that may take time we don't have. This briefing is to pass on what we know and help me decide what to do about it."

The briefing was short and to the point. Brother Sam's bass voice, contrasting with his small frame, rang out through the room. He pointed to a large map on a white board, and started off with the usual introduction.

"Our area of responsibility is Arizona and parts of the surrounding states, although teams are often sent all over the country, and sometimes the world. Current situation: Arizona is being invaded. We had reports from other areas of witches on the move and the sightings by our own scouts and off-duty Hammers who were vectored in to observe. There are now seven groups we've positively identified, down from eleven earlier."

There was some muttering at this.

That's impossible, I thought. *There can't be that many.* In two years, I'd only seen maybe ten witches, and most of those were solitary.

Brother Sam's voice interrupted my thoughts. "At any given time there are only two to three witches here in Arizona, but now that number has gone up at least fivefold. There've already been a few battles. Some were inconclusive skirmishes, others an annihilation. Losers have fled. They are being tracked and once captured, the witches will be interrogated for information and then Purged. That may take time we don't have. The town of Antelope has already been the victim of a 'bizarre natural disaster.' The travel routes used by the witches are all from the north, east, and west. The team sent south hasn't reported in yet.

"What we need is more information," said Brother Sam, after a pause. "The witches aren't targeting us. They're keeping well away from the monastery. According to our sources, none of the witches are within fifty miles of our location. They're here for something, but it's not us."

There was silence for a minute before the questions began. The usual answer was a version of "I don't know."

While no one was afraid to do their duty, going out blind was usually unnecessarily dangerous. The Hammers were stoic, not fatalistic. No one was looking for a glorious death. Tension rose in the room every time Brother Sam couldn't give a satisfactory reply. Mutters and hushed conversations broke out. Brother Sam was sweating under the onslaught of probing questions and his inability to give complete answers.

Finally, the Master Hammer stood. "Thank you, Brother Sam. That's all for now."

Brother Sam took his seat, obviously grateful.

Hammers come in two distinct sizes: normal like me, but looking very small in comparison to our large Brothers. The Master Hammer, Brother Michael, was of the large variety, and then some. "Massive" was really the only word to describe him physically. It was rumored he'd played football professionally when he was younger, but that was stated very quietly and thirdhand, in a "someone told someone who told me" kind of way. The Master Hammer never talked about his past when he instructed a class. Like me, he wore a ring on his left ring finger, indicating he'd Purged a Screwface singlehandedly. On the few occasions we'd spoken, I hadn't dared ask how he got his, and no one who knew was talking. Brother Michael was also the only man I'd ever met who could wear a ponytail and not look effeminate. The blond-turning-to-gray ponytail gave him a Bronze Age warrior king look. He had a slight limp when he walked, though that didn't slow him down. I'd seen him shirtless once, and his torso was a mass of scars from various blades and claws, bullet holes, and even a burn running down one side. I worried that, in a few years, my body would look the same, and my eyes would hold the same world-crushing weariness.

"I believe we must take to the field," he said. No one spoke, or even seemed to move. He swiveled his head slowly, taking in the room. "Yes, I know. Seven groups of witches may be more than we can handle, and if they combine, even just long enough to attack a common enemy, we may all fail." He paused to let this sink in before continuing. "We don't know why they're here, but we need to find out. We need to be in a position to stop them, and we can't do that here, waiting for more information. Historically, when witches band together, it's to try to unleash something even more hideous and destructive than themselves. This might be a summoning or an attempt to start a plague. Does everyone remember the Hanta outbreak in '95?"

There were blanched faces and hesitant nods from some of the proctors.

"Hiding behind walls is not the Hammer way. I've already sent out a request for assistance, both to other Hammer Priories and to other Inquisitors. It may be hours or days, depending on how far they have to come, and by then, they may be too late to do anything.

"I'm declaring a mass graduation, for all students in their last phase, regardless of completion of their final exercise. The remaining students will be used as auxiliaries if they're physically capable."

Several monks, and not just students, traded glances at this news. I breathed out a sigh, not of excitement, but dread. I was going back into battle. Part of me was ready to prove myself, to show Bishop Bathoie, and Brother Otto, and the others that I was worthy, that they'd made a mistake in sending me away. A smaller part was still unsure.

He turned to us, paused a moment as though considering something, and continued, "Hammers, go get your brands, gear up, and be ready to join your teams."

The brand was just that. Each successful graduate was branded with a stylized cross on their right hip that looked more like a hammer. I didn't really care to get one, but nobody had asked my opinion, and I wasn't stupid enough to share it with the others.

CHAPTER 16

Just prior to my branding, we had a very short induction ceremony that was mostly a blur. The Master Hammer led the ceremony, asking God to keep us pure and receive us into his arms when we fell.

Cheery stuff, I thought.

Thoughts like that are why you couldn't stay in New England, mocked my darker voice. I'd gotten better at shutting it up, but it did get in the occasional zinger.

I refocused on the ceremony. The students knelt in front of the altar in the transept, the area between the first set of pews and the dais where the priest stood during mass. More prayers were said, we were asked if we accepted our new mandate, to "Purge the world of the most vile Screwfaces and their minions until age or death takes you." Once we accepted, we stood up, turned around, and were introduced as Hammers. Fast, dark, and brutal, that was the Hammer way.

I only winced slightly as the brand cooked my skin—I'd been in worse pain. The resident medic, a former RN with Popeye-sized forearms, attached my bandage with all the tenderness of a punch.

"No matter what, do not let this stay on more than two days. Try not to rub it, even if it itches, and if you start to smell something funny, come running."

"Yeah, no problem," I said.

That's going to take off a lot of hair when the time comes.

When he was done, I put on my gear. It took a few adjustments, but I was able to get my kit not to rub directly on the brand by loosening straps and shifting things around. I went back to the briefing room to find my team assignment and finish getting outfitted. When I walked in, the tables held various collections of gear, ammo, maps, batteries, and spare parts in random heaps. Again, there was silence for the most part. Back in my apprentice days, there would've been more banter and laughing; here, there was the occasional hushed voice and silent intensity that the Hammers seemed to possess in unlimited supply. When I went to the board that listed team assignments, I couldn't find my name. I double checked, but it wasn't there. I looked around, perplexed.

What the hell? I did everything I was supposed to. I've got the brand. Is there yet another test I have to pass?

Teams were forming up or moving out, and there didn't seem to be any empty spots or people waiting for one of the new guys to show up. I started to move, to ask one of the team leaders or captains, when I saw Brother Malachi. He was fully outfitted, and ready for a Purge.

"Brother, it's good to see you again," I said, and I meant it.

He took me into a one-armed man hug. "Sebastian, it's very good to see you as well." We broke the hug, and he looked me in the eyes. "I hope you've learned a few things here."

"I have, and more than just a few things. I think I'm much better prepared and more able to do what needs to be done." It was half-true. I was in much better shape than when I was an apprentice, I had more knowledge, and was better at fighting and using weapons. Still, I wasn't sure if I was ready, if I could get my head into the game.

"And the important lessons, how are those?"

I knew what he meant: not the curriculum, but the healing. I started with the easy answer. "My hearing is the same. Music still eludes me, so my violin playing is off..." Thaddeus's attempt to break me still lingered. The neurosurgeon had told me it could take years before I got anywhere. It was even possible I would never be able to understand music again. Not hearing what I was doing, not understanding the sounds I made was infuriating. I'd wanted to smash the thing many times, but I kept at it. I'd made Sarah's memory a promise.

Brother Malachi's eyes seemed to water, and his mouth turned down in a small frown. He was silent for a moment, and I dropped my eyes. He asked in a shaky voice, "Have you come to forgive yourself and learn peace?"

"I try," I said, still looking down. "I try so hard, but she haunts me in my dreams. She never forgives me. And I have doubts."

He gave a small, sad sigh. "I see that telling you it wasn't your fault, that you're not doomed to Hell, and that you're on the sides of angels isn't going to work, so I guess what I need to know is should you go on this Purge or should you stay back?"

I looked up quickly, staring at his face. This was a man who'd accepted me when all others had cast me out. He'd stayed with me, mentored and prayed with me as I healed. Used his connections to get me into training, where things were structured and I didn't have time to dwell on my past. I was much better, more capable than when I'd left New England.

I will not fail.

"I'm ready."

He peered at me, presumably looking for weakness or hesitation. After a moment, he nodded. "Good, you're with me." He handed me gear from the tables, and I put it on mechanically.

"I thought I was going to be a part of a Hammer team."

"Think again. You're too good for that. I needed you to get better, needed you trained to a higher standard, and that meant Hammer training. I didn't send you here to waste your time fighting Screwfaces. There's worse out there, and that's what we hunt."

I was flabbergasted. I'd met most of the Hammers here, and I was in awe of their martial abilities. Any of them could outshoot me. Most could beat me up like a sick five-year-old girl. I wasn't in their league. I was a lot closer than when I'd started, but it would be years before I was ready. I also hadn't missed what he'd said. What could be worse than a Screwface, and why didn't I know about it already? I just stood there, unable to think straight.

Seeing me mentally flap, Brother Malachi grabbed my left hand and held it up at eye level. "See the ring?"

I nodded dumbly.

"How many in your class have one?"

"Just me."

"So do you think you might be a bit better prepared than the rest of your classmates?"

"Well yeah, but..." I shifted uncomfortably, glancing around, not meeting his eyes. I saw Brother Greg link up with three other Hammers to go through pre-combat checks of each other's gear. He had a big smile on his face.

"No buts. There are Hammers here that have never earned this ring. Never. They've been Purging Screwfaces for twenty or more years, and have never handled one solo. Now you have one. Why? Not because you were lucky, not because she walked into the bullets, but because you're good. You don't fold under pressure. Even when scared, when faced with the horror that's out there, you keep going. That's why you didn't have to repeat a single class. You never gave up."

It was a pep talk, probably just to make me feel better and nothing more, but it worked. Part of me knew I was being manipulated, but it worked. I visualized all those times during my training when it got hard, when I wanted to quit, but I never did. Even when sick or injured, I kept going.

"Oh," I said, realization hitting me. I'd never been very athletic before my apprentice training. I was a scientist, a chemist; I exercised my brain. Being smart was easy for me, being good at something physical was new.

"Starting to get it now? Stop the false modesty crap, it's annoying. God gave you talents. Use them."

Acceptance set in, but doubts lingered. Still, now was not the time to be weak. There was no way I was going to let him down, not after everything he'd done for me. "All right, so what's the plan?"

"We're a team of two. We get the full outfit and some extra ammo. We'll be flankers, and then, if the situation changes, we'll be assault or, heaven forbid, blockers."

I nodded. Blockers were there to cut off retreat, flankers would come from the side, and assault was just that. Still, that gave us generic positions, not the important where or who. "That's pretty vague. Do we have more on where and what we're facing?"

"Partially. We're going south-west. There are at least two groups where we're heading. The scout thinks one is a necromancer, and the other...they're not sure if she's a sorceress or what. They're headed toward each other, and with luck, we'll reach them after they've fought for a bit and are easier to deal with."

"That's the plan? Drive to the sounds of fighting and finish off what's left?"

"Pretty much. We'll be getting updates as we take the field, so we can refine as we go." Seeing my worried look, he laughed. "Relax. We'll be drawing up plans on the way down, and we're going with two other teams. This isn't a berserker mission. It's just that time isn't on our side, so we'll have to improvise. A lot." With that, he gave another laugh and led me to a waiting vehicle.

CHAPTER 17

Brother Malachi and I were in the last bench seats of a large SUV. The Hammers in front of us talked quietly, passing maps and papers back and forth, working on the details of the mission. The Hammer in the front passenger seat was either on the radio or his cellphone, getting more information or passing along reports. We had another SUV in our convoy, which held another team.

"Okay," said Brother Malachi, "here's the thing. We're only two people, but we're doing the job of four, so you have to keep from fixating in one direction. It's too easy to get flanked or taken from the rear if you over-focus on the front. If we're moving, I want you to look back every third step."

"And if we're waiting?"

"Use this," he said and handed me a small, flat electronic clock. "It's set to go off every fifteen seconds, but only vibrate, so put it in an inside pocket of your gear where you'll feel it." When I was done, he handed me an incredibly detailed map. "We're going to start here," he said, pointing. It wasn't even a town, just a collection of old houses near the New Mexico border. "Keep at right angles to the assault team. We'll flank the bad guys so they're taking fire from two sides. That'll make it more difficult for them to focus on one direction and kill our team members." He leaned into me, staring hard. "Try not to stop. Keep a slow, steady pace unless we get a call for pursuit, which is unlikely. The guys in front are the assault. They set up here and move this way." He brought up one hand and make a walking motion with two fingers going from north to south on the map. "The blockers will be positioned here." He pointed at the map again and drew an east-west line on it with one finger. "The idea is to force the witches away from cover and into our ambush. The blockers will have the shotguns, which should effectively deal with any problems."

The clock vibrated, and I almost turned my head to look back.

Brother Malachi was too confident, too cavalier, and I didn't like it. I preferred methodical plans—this was going off half-cocked at best.

A voice in my head was yelling,

That's it? That's the plan? Go in like this is a John Woo movie? Shoot anything moving, and hope we survive?

"Brother Malachi, I understand we don't have a lot of time, but can we get some recon, or intel, or just…more, before we go in guns blazing? How many minions? Any followers? Are there civilians? What about cops? Where are the rally points, medical pick up…?"

His face was reddening, his mouth twisting into a snarl. I wanted to scoot back, to get away before he struck me. "Are you refusing?" he asked in a raspy voice.

That took me by surprise. I didn't think we could refuse a mission. I shook my head to deal with the angry Brother in front of me. "Um... No. Of course not. I just want to go in with as much info as possible. We seem to be ignoring all the reconnaissance instructions we had in training and acting like an old west posse." Brother Malachi's face changed rapidly, and he laughed. "Oh, that's good," he said between laughs. "An old west posse, I like that. I'm glad you still have your sense of humor. We'll need it."

The Hammers glanced back a time or two at the noise, but didn't say anything.

It took him a minute to calm down, but I didn't mind waiting. I was just happy he was no longer angry.

"Okay, Sebastian," he said, wiping his eyes, "that was your last test. I wanted to see if you were too scared to do your job or too ready to die. I gave you a half-assed plan to see if you'd back out or just accept it blindly. You did neither. You're right where you need to be, attitude-wise."

"Oh," I said dumbly. Once again, I got the feeling there were plans within plans, and I was still asleep.

Brother Malachi just chuckled to himself and waited.

I felt too stupid for not realizing he was testing me to get angry. "So there's a decent plan and some recon?"

"Yep, we have eyes on our target. Intel teams have been shadowing each group. Some of the teams have had eyes on for hours, others almost a day. We still have two groups—a necromancer and a sorceress. They're close to each other, but not together. Remember, two different types of witches don't form a coven. Their interests and motivations clash. They're not traveling together, nor have they fought. Best we can tell, there's a temporary truce between them, but how long that will last is anyone's guess."

"Do we know the types of minions these witches have?"

"The necromancer has a construct, a re-animation, and a small group of lichs. The sorceress has a large group of fanatics with her and an imp on a leash."

That made sense. Necromancers favor lichs over other types of minions, and sorceresses do love an entourage and their "pets." The re-animation was a worry. I'd studied them but never dealt with one.

"What's a re-animation like to deal with for real?" I asked.

"Resistant to magic, like an ogre. No free will. Bigger than Muscle, slower than a werewolf. It'll take a lot to stop one, but it can be done."

The only dealings I'd had with an ogre was running from one when I was in the hospital. It was huge, and seemed impervious to bullets. Even hit by a shotgun blasts multiple times, the ogre had kept coming. I only escaped because it couldn't run as fast as we could drive the stolen ambulance.

Now that we were on the actual mission, I wasn't nervous about facing something that tough, but I wanted to be as prepared as possible. "Any weak spots, other than the head?"

"Holy water, of course," said Brother Malachi. "They're also not very bright. They tend to charge in straight lines, and they move fast but have a tough time turning or dealing with a new situation, so be prepared to bound back at an angle."

"What about the imp? I've only seen the internalized ones."

"External imps are essentially the same as internal but they don't live in the witch. They're given a cat or other small animal to eat, which also binds them here. Small animal, small imp, less power. And if the imp consumes the entire animal, it can break the binding. If it escapes before the witch is prepared, the imp does whatever evil it can as payback."

"Why?"

"It's a bit insulting. First they're stuck in hell being abused and abusing weaker creatures, trying to barter and claw their way up in power then suddenly they're brought back to Earth, which must be much nicer, but they've changed. They like Hell, they're used to it. Earth hurts them. Reminds them of what they had and threw away. And they're trapped here. Forced to do the bidding of a lesser mind."

"Lesser mind?"

"No one summons an oracle that knows less than they do. What would be the point?"

"Oh. Well, can't they refuse?"

"Nope. To be able to say no, you have to have free will. To have free will, you have to have a soul, something they lost a long time ago. They're trapped here until released. Usually by the death of the witch."

"So why would a witch ever have an external imp?"

"Mostly for power. The witch can't control the rate of decay with an internal imp. With an external imp, there's less power, but the witch is also less likely to be consumed in the end. Perhaps she's afraid of becoming a puppet." He leaned back with a grim smile. "Or it could be vanity, hubris. The witch thinks she's so powerful, no imp could ever escape. Or maybe the imp has convinced her it's loyal to the summoner and would never harm her. Take your pick."

"The imp wouldn't harm her? People fall for that?"

"Since the dawn of time," he replied softly.

Another thought occurred to me; after all, we were Hammers. "Do we have any Screwfaces moving about or do we know what other types of witches we might be facing?"

Brother Malachi called out to the Hammer team leader. "Brother Seth, do we have any reports of Screwfaces? Any news on other types of witches out there besides this sorceress and necromancer?"

The driver stayed focused on the road, but all the other Hammers stopped what they were doing and looked at Brother Malachi like he'd just sworn during Mass.

Then Brother Seth glanced back, held up a finger and repeated the question to the person on the other end of the phone. He nodded a few times then, removing the phone from his ear, turned back to us. "There was a single spotting of a Screwface earlier," he said, "but the team wasn't able to get into position in time to follow her, and she disappeared. The rest who haven't been defeated or absorbed seem to be necromancers. There's the sorceress we're trying to intercept and one unknown.

That's not all of them, but we should be getting more in a bit. There's an update every half-hour if you want to listen in."

"Thank you, Brother, but no," said Brother Malachi.

The Hammers seemed to relax and go back to their quiet discussion.

Brother Malachi turned back to me, making sure I'd heard.

"Why so many necromancers?" I asked.

He shrugged. "Dunno. This is new to me too. If it's a summoning, any type can do that. It's weird to have mixed types together. I guess it's possible that the sorceress is also a necromancer, but unlikely."

"I thought that only males, warlocks, could be more than one type."

"I've never heard of a witch being more than one type, but there's a lot we don't know about witches and their hows and whys. Anything's possible. It is, after all, called magic."

I glanced down for a moment. It was gently delivered, but I still felt foolish.

One of the Hammers handed Brother Malachi another map. We spent the rest of the time going over formations, fall back areas, signals, expected responses, and the like.

CHAPTER 18

James

I drove into a war zone, one of the most beautiful sights imaginable. Bodies were scattered about the battlefield—some burned, some sliced into pieces, and others partially chewed. The afterimages of magic blazed here and there, visible to those with eyes and acceptance.

I sighed mentally.

If only Olivia could've been something more, I mused then stopped that thought hard. *This is no time to be weak or sentimental. What's done is done. She would never make it through the transformation.* The sun was getting lower, but the desert was still hot and—good for what I was doing—empty. In the last two hours, I'd only seen one pickup truck heading the other way. The driver, like most in the area, was wearing a cowboy hat and sunglasses, along with the slack expression of the mentally weak.

Stupid cattle, I thought as we passed each other. *Wonder what he'll do when he sees Yun. Probably try to be heroic and end up dying messily.*

It was a shame I couldn't be there to watch his eyes go wide when he realized he was going to die, hear his screams, and feel his blood on my skin...but I had more important matters to accomplish.

I made another turn onto another empty road, heading closer to the hills where the house was located. Just after the turn, fresh skid marks on the road crisscrossed the pavement, and finally veered off to one side. The three-strand barbed-wire fence, meant to keep in cattle, hadn't stood a chance. The RV was fifty feet from the road and parallel to it, resting on its rims. A small caravan of junker cars had encircled it like a pack of wolves around a moose. Two of the cars had been flipped and one, while upright, burned an unnatural purple-black.

Another fight. Perhaps another opportunity.

Any survivors would probably be weak. I slowed, coasting along to see if anyone remained or if I'd have to fight the victor. It was quiet and there were no flashes of magic or motion.

I let the car come to a stop, but left it running. I waited, looking for movement, but all was still. Sure that the fight was over and any survivors were fleeing as fast as they could, I got out. Keeping the car between myself and the RV, I prepared. The MP-5 was in one hand and the severed hand in my other. With a single thought, I called forth the magic contained within, ready in case there were any predators still about. I moved quickly from the car to the RV, carefully scanning the area for a trap. The need for information and possible loot outweighed the risk of another battle, but I couldn't linger. I couldn't get too diverted from my main task of preventing Thaddeus's revenge.

The ground was blackened in several spots, and rocks and cacti were strewn about. I walked warily past a cluster of bodies that had died messily. Each one was quite large.

"Muscle," I said as I approached. Another low level minion. Someone was fighting out of their weight class. With stakes this high, minions of this caliber were fit for sacrifice only.

Past them was the RV, and I slowed down, listening and alert for anything out of place. The susurration of the wind was the only sound. The insects and other animals were quiet, hoping to avoid becoming prey themselves. Once at the RV, I kept close to it without actually touching the side, and made my way around the back. I stopped when I got to the corner and did a last check of my surroundings. Nothing moved except the wind, but now I could smell the coppery tang of blood. The main battle had taken place here, out of sight of the road. The area hummed with energy, and reeked of death. Breathing in deeply at the smell, I had a smile on my lips as I enjoyed the familiar tingles of magic and blood.

Ready for whatever would come next, I took a quick peek, ducking my head around and then back. There were two groups a few yards apart and obviously on different sides. Only one figure stood, and I focused on the first threat. An animated black metal parody of a human shape, it was composed of articulated tubes, topped with a fleshless skull. The metallic teeth didn't gleam but seemed to draw in the light like a series of black holes turned into a set of dentures. The eyes were greenish gems that burned as though on fire. It wore what looked like a crash cymbal from a drum set as a hat, tilted at a jaunty angle. The clockwork, a rare and powerful minion, stood over a prostrate form. It wasn't moving yet, and I glanced at the other pile...and almost stepped back.

A huge, hairy shape sat on the ground, holding something in its lap. I slowly edged forward and peered more intently. The hairy shape was what was left of a gorilla. It had been chopped and slashed many times, but still lived. A growing pond of blood, the size of a kiddie pool, circled the creature and what it held. A powerful animalistic witch must've been controlling it, but in the end it hadn't been enough. Warily easing closer, I could make out more details through the blood and gore. The witch herself lay in its lap. The gorilla was stroking its former mistress's head with one huge black paw—the other was missing, lost in the fight. The stump bled in slow spurts. The witch's head had been wrenched around, and the rest of her looked squeezed. Broken bones jutted here and there from her skin. While her head was on the gorilla's lap, the rest of her was sprawled out, limbs bent in wrong directions, in the spreading blood. The gorilla saw me and bared its fangs, but then it shuddered and its eyes dimmed and went out. Its head sank down on its massive chest.

I came out from around the corner completely to deal with the clockwork, which stood guard over its former master. The warlock must've still been alive as the clockwork hadn't reverted to inert metal yet. It held two swords and raised them at the sight of me. I poured power into the hand and severed the clockwork's connection with the dying warlock, transferring it to myself. A clockwork could take years to create, but control was easy, especially as its owner lay dying. I could almost see the tether snap and rush into my body.

As I scanned the area to make sure no one else was still around or alive, information sped into me from the clockwork. It was called Glaive, a good name, and it had been created two years prior by its master, Roberto, who'd struggled for a decade to master the lore and metalwork necessary to bring it to life.

Not just a basic brass or bronze clockwork like the ones I'd heard about, Glaive was smelted from iron—much stronger, and more dangerous to its master's enemies. Roberto, not satisfied with merely making a stronger minion, had made one smarter as well. He'd imprisoned a minor metal spirit inside Glaive to give it self-awareness and the ability to follow complex instructions, like driving the RV.

Clever Midas.

Midases were forever tinkering with machines, semi-organic creations, and metals. Handy, I supposed, but Midases weren't usually very strong and had to resort to trading their creations for protection. Roberto must've been an exception. He had his own minor demesne in Colorado where he tinkered and carried out his research. Roberto did trade his knowledge, and occasionally some of his toys, but as an equal, not as a subject or as part of his rent. He'd been content to stay there, until one of his instruments sensed the scream of Thaddeus's return and backtracked it. Seeing the chance for more power, Roberto had come searching before he was ready.

Foolish, I thought, as the information kept pouring in.

They'd been in the RV when they were attacked. Roberto may have been clever, but he was no battle warlock. He'd sent Glaive to deal with the Muscle, who were just a sacrificial distraction, and the gorilla had circled around and attacked from a flank. Despite being crushed by eight-hundred pounds of animal fury, Roberto hung on and struck at the witch when she got close. Glaive easily dealt with the gorilla until called back to guard. Roberto must've been hoping to heal fast enough to live. He would've, if given time, but that had just run out. I was impressed enough not to let Roberto linger. I took his grimoire and had Glaive finish him off.

CHAPTER 19

Sebastian

Things were tense but calm until we ran into a trio of witches doing their best to kill each other. "Contact. Contact," squawked the radio.

There was a brief pause in the SUV and our heads turned to the radio in the middle of the dashboard, as we all processed what had just been said. Pens, maps, and reference sheets were cast aside to litter the floor of our SUV—along with our plans for a systematic ambush. Like all plans, they were great until you actually met the enemy and had to improvise.

Weapons that had been checked and rechecked were given one last glance, just in case. Ear buds were fitted and our personnel radios began to yammer information. I tuned it out. At the moment, I was just a foot soldier, and if that was my role, I was determined to be the best. The extra information would only confuse me. My job was to stick to Brother Malachi like a lamprey, back him up, and watch our flanks. My heart sped up, and I could feel my temperature rise in anticipation of what was next. I tried to remain calm and breathe deeply to control the excitement and not let it overwhelm me.

The driver went faster to catch up to the first SUV, and the rest of us got ready to unload. The Hammers next to the doors each had a hand on the handles, ready to burst out the moment we stopped or slowed enough. While the SUVs were roomy and got us from A to B, they were easy targets. Not mobile armored bunkers, they were scant protection from bullets, explosions, fire, and magic.

Glad I'm not a driver.

He would be stuck in the vehicle until it was over, hoping the fight didn't come to him unexpectedly. I don't think I could handle just sitting there while my team-mates went into action. Listening to their cries as they gave orders and information to each other, their screams as they died one by one until it was just me, trapped, listening to static, waiting for what came next.

Whoa. I gave myself a shake. *Get your shit together. Stop the morbid crap.*

I focused on what I'd been taught to do once I exited. We needed to clear the vehicle as fast as we could, and then get away from the SUV. A race-walk pace, a little less than a jog. Movement—rapid, controlled movement—would be our protection and get us safely away to maneuver into position. Flank the enemy. Sow confusion about the direction of our attack. Hit them where they didn't expect it. Rapidly overwhelm them, as we couldn't stand toe-to-toe with a witch and win.

"Two o'clock!" yelled the driver, giving us the general direction of the battle.

At the same time, he jammed on the brakes and slewed the car to a stop. The driver hunched behind the nearly non-existent protection of the steering column. The purple-black of magic flashed through the windows, and the sick smell of burned rubber filled my nostrils. Doors popped open, and Hammers exited in a rush.

Brother Malachi and I tumbled out of the back, taking our backpacks with us and hunching over to make ourselves a smaller target. Spots of snarling, snapping purple-black shot past us like unholy fireworks. A purple-black manta-ray-like figure with a broken wing wafted past, getting lower and lower until it plowed into the ground with a wet flop. My stomach roiled in response to seeing magic again. The stench of it coated my nostrils like a scummy oil. I wanted to spit the taste out, but knew it wouldn't do any good. With a faint buzzing sound, more pieces of not-light went by in a corkscrewing fashion, boring holes through an innocent cactus.

As revolting and fascinating as the light show was, I kept my focus on Brother Malachi, watching to see which way we'd go. We paused in the middle of the road and knelt down, awaiting instructions.

"Flankers take left. Be ready in three minutes," came over the radio just as my knee hit the warm and hard road.

"Roger," said Brother Malachi as we moved out.

After scuttling the rest of the way across the road, we came to a barbed-wire fence and crossed it. The backpacks were determined to catch and slow us down, forcing us to struggle with the strands for a few seconds.

The buzzer almost made me jump when it went off. I took a quick look around and saw no threats.

Yet, I thought darkly.

We'd only taken a few dozen more steps when we wheeled off to one side and, at a rapid trot, made a wide loop in the direction the spells had come from.

Gotta maintain control. Gotta get into position to support the main effort.

They'd give us time to get into position, but not forever. The buzzer seemed to go off at random, startling me each time.

Three minutes, I thought, not sure if it was too long or not enough, *that's a lifetime. I can run more than a half mile in three minutes. I could fire off all my ammo. The assault element could be completely overrun and killed.*

The buzzer went off again, snapping me out of my thoughts. I looked back and, seeing nothing, concentrated on more positive ideas.

We can do this. I will not fail.

I glanced up, looking for reassurance, but other than blue sky and a small cloud, I saw nothing to confirm my prayers. I had to have faith.

Essentially, we were winging it. This was a movement to contact action, an event where two opposing forces bumped into each other and started fighting. No plan, no strategy, just savage force and the desire to live.

This felt like a frontal charge. There was nothing to hide behind, to use for protection. Part of me loved it—a chance to really make my mark—but another warned me this was a fast way to find out just how nice heaven was this time of year.

Keep moving, I thought to Brother Malachi, willing him to continue. *They can't hit us if we don't stop.*

He didn't even slow down, his thick legs stomping along, propelling him forward, as I trailed along in his wake. His MP-5, like mine, was up and ready, and as his head moved, so did the weapon, tracking, ready to fire. I was protecting our right side, glancing back every few steps to make sure nothing crept up behind us.

"Frag," someone shouted over the radio.

I dived for the ground as I'd done many, many times in training. As I came down, I glanced at Brother Malachi so I knew where he was and wouldn't inadvertently fire my weapon in his direction. Our eyes locked, and he gave me a fleeting smile. I craned my head back, looking over my shoulder, making sure the desert was still empty behind us while we waited for the crump of the explosion. My gear dug into me, and my brand itched. When the explosion subsided, we were back up, weapons tracking, scanning for targets, and running for a small hill that hid the battle from us. Normally we would've eased up the hill, moving slowly to get to a good ambush position, but the grenade had changed everything. They knew we were here, and would turn on us quickly. We had to flank the witches before our main attackers were overwhelmed.

We crested the hill to a tableau that would've made Bosch give up absinthe and sing hymns in church for the rest of his life. Brother Malachi glanced at me then back, his eyes wide, and said over the radio, "Crap."

Two witches and one warlock were doing their damnedest to kill each other with their minions in a three-way battle. One set of minions looked like a type of harpy, with a woman's upper body and bottom halves feathered in a flesh color. Their legs were chicken-like and orange-ish. In each hand, they held a short whip or riding crop, which glowed a malevolent red and sizzled when swung. I vaguely remembered seeing a picture and description of them in one of our monster classes, but couldn't remember anything about them beyond that. I had no idea what kind of witch used them, or for what purpose.

Another set of minions looked like humans who'd been drowned then left out to rot. Their skin was green, loose, and ill-fitting, and they scuttled more than walked. Their hands were claw-like, their nails dirt-encrusted. I knew their eyes would be yellow, and they'd reek of the graveyard. They were lichs—bodies brought back from the dead, with their intellects intact, to serve a necromancer.

The last was a single minion, a construct. Vaguely human-shaped but about eight feet tall, it was composed of different body parts stolen from an unconsecrated grave and reanimated. Naked, and sexless, it bulged with muscles. It held a two-headed battle-axe in one meaty paw. It was yelling, or maybe singing, and displaying a feral smile. The misshapen face almost appeared happy.

The witches and warlock were a bit back from the brawl, shooting spells at hapless minions and each other. Spells bounced off the construct and flew in all directions, striking other minions and causing the witches and warlock to dodge. A small tornado, about five feet tall and made of purple-black light, skittered across the road, tossing lichs and the bird women aside. The pavement sizzled in several spots, and in one long furrow, it was just gone, replaced by what looked like frozen

110

puke. The air reeked of dead flesh and mildew, making my stomach quiver. The not-light of magic hurt to look at, and I had to keep my eyes moving.

The construct snatched one of the lichs off the ground when it got too close, and used it like a rotten club. The lich plowed into one of the harpies mid-air, crashing her back to the ground, pulverizing both bodies and producing a shower of fluid and bones to splash everything nearby. At the same time, the construct swung the axe in a broad motion, catching two other lichs. They burst apart like balloons filled with rotten blood.

A single shot from a high-powered rifle rang out, and then another. It was our cue that the advance had begun. A sniper team had set up and managed to take out one of the harpies—though how they were able to get a good shot in the maelstrom of moving bodies, flashing magic, and showers of blood, I hadn't a clue. I was just going to shoot into the mass of the scrum until I got closer.

The clock vibrated again. I glanced over my right shoulder; it was still clear. The assault team had formed up in a line on the road.

"Advance," came over the radio, and the battle was on.

CHAPTER 20

Brother Malachi and I moved forward, using aimed shots timed with each step. The witches and warlock must've seen their minions dropping, because they turned toward the assault team. The little tornado guttered out as they stared at the line of monks advancing toward them. I guess they were assessing us and figuring out what to do next. Brother Malachi and I kept advancing and firing. One of the witches broke first, leaving her minions, trying to escape. She only got a few steps before she was tackled by a lich. The lich's talons flashed, and chunks of her back were scraped off and shoved into its mouth. The second witch lifted her hands to the sky and summoned a huge ball of flames. Faces, hideously deformed, appeared on the surface as though the ball were constructed of severed heads that had been stretched and melted. Blood-red flames wavered, expanding and contracting on their own. A wail, the sound of an animal in pain, emanated from the ball.

She launched it in the direction of the battle. The fireball streaked through the air, shrieking the whole time, landing on the scrum of minions. Several caught fire and ran screaming. The fireball bounced toward the advancing assault team, who had to dive underneath it to avoid being consumed. It sailed over and past them, bouncing along a few more time before exploding. Flaming shards, roughly the size and shape of a human head, flew everywhere. A piece hit one of the team, and he lit up like a roman candle. He didn't even have time to scream. The others had to scramble away as his ammo cooked off and his grenades exploded. The body was flung into the air, tumbling end over end until finally landing flat and in several clumps. The remaining faces bounced along until they came to a stop, the mouths trying to bite and rend without effect, before melting into the ground. The assault team picked themselves up and moved toward the remaining witches. The surviving minions were on fire, apart from the construct.

The warlock must've seen Brother Malachi and me. He turned and pointed at us, saying something. The construct turned and ran toward us. It had stopped singing, but still had an insane smile on its face.

"Full auto," screamed Brother Malachi. He flipped the selector switch on his weapon and opened up on the construct. I did the same. We had maybe a hundred yards between us and the raging battle. The construct was gathering momentum and moving fast.

"Mag," shouted Brother Malachi, dropping the old one and fumbling in a fresh one. I used short, choppy bursts, aiming for the head and top of the torso until I ran out as well.

"Mag," I yelled as I hit the magazine release and traded out the empty.

"Bound back," commanded Brother Malachi.

Turning the way we'd come, I ran five longs steps then faced back. I sighted on the construct and opened fire. It was getting closer very fast. The smoke and heat of my weapon stung my eyes, making me blink. Brother Malachi moved out, stomping past me. The bolt of my MP-5 locked open just as Brother Malachi began to fire. By this time, the construct had come halfway to us, its axe getting larger by the second. Pulling out the spent magazine, I bounded back to just over the top of the hill, next to Brother Malachi. My mind screamed for me to keep going, but I ignored it.

I slapped in a full magazine and took aim, still concentrating on the top third of the torso, hoping for a kill shot. Hoping to splatter its rotten brains out into the desert. My stomach churned, my eyes were still watering, and a scream welled up inside me. The construct let out a keening wail. Brother Malachi had managed to take out one eye, but it still ran toward us. My magazine quickly went dry, and the construct was so close now, I was sure I could feel the ground tremble.

"Fall back," commanded Brother Malachi again.

I spun and ran down the small hill, taking a few extra steps so I'd have a clear field of fire. I switched magazines and yelled, "Go," into my radio.

Brother Malachi did a twisting dive from the crest of the hill, sliding down in a semi-controlled fall. The construct appeared right after him, stopping for a moment. It was backlit and just a few yards away. For a second, it looked around stupidly, trying to find its target. Seeing me, the construct raised the axe and howled again. I squeezed the trigger, aiming for the neck and head. Bits of rotten flesh rippled and peeled away under the bullet impacts. Despite the damage, it continued, taking another step toward me. Brother Malachi got up on one knee and began firing as well. I could see its face clearly now—skin had been torn away, and its lower jaw was gone. Flames danced and burned as the silver of our bullets made contact with the magical flesh of the construct. And still it came for me.

The construct took another step, and then another, once again picking up speed as it strode after us. Brother Malachi and I continued to fire, trying to hit something vital, trying to stop it, but with no effect. The axe came up high, blood and other substances dripping off slowly, and in a few more steps, it would be in range. When that axe came down, I'd be dead. I wanted to run so badly.

It took another step, and its arm dropped to the ground, the hand still grasping the axe. The stitches holding the forearm to the upper arm had unraveled. It stopped moving and stared at the stump, grunting almost as though it were confused. Instead of the usual arterial spurt, an oily reddish fluid dripped slowly from the severed limb.

I was so surprised, I stopped shooting at it for a second and started to lower my weapon.

"Keep firing," said Brother Malachi, "it's not dead yet."

The construct howled again, but it was softer, almost as though the creature were in pain. I brought my weapon up, but more stitches popped free and body parts disassociated from each other, collapsing into a smelly, twitching pile of limbs. The head bounced past me then rolled to a stop and rocked in place, eyes blinking and mouth trying to make a sound.

I gave Brother Malachi a *what the Hell?* look. He was busy listening to the radio and held up a finger.

"Sebastian killed the construct. We're doing a quick clean up over the hill," he said over the radio.

I heard the affirmative to proceed.

Brother Malachi focused on me. "I guess the others killed the warlock. Good for us. Not so good for the mission." He pulled a fresh magazine from his combat vest and swapped it with the one in his weapon as he stood up. He walked over to the axe and kicked the arm toward the pile. It landed with a *splat*. "Change mags," he reminded me.

"Not so good for the mission?" I repeated stupidly as I switched out.

He gave me a sharp look, eyes boring into me for a second. "You guard, I'll explain," he said. He knelt down, and shrugged off his backpack as I looked around at the empty desert, still confused.

"It fell apart because the spell died, which means, most likely, the team killed the warlock," he repeated while I looked out at the emptiness around us. "Dead warlock means no information, and we need to know more. Why was he here? What's going on?" There was a pause, and I glanced at him. He'd stopped rifling through his backpack and was looking directly at me. "Kick the head over to me, please."

You should've figured that out, idiot, I berated myself as I did what he asked.

The head was starting to smoke and shrink. I reared a leg back, aimed, and put it right on top of the heap of body parts. By now, the pile was also smoking and melting, giving off a horrid stench.

Brother Malachi had removed a large canteen from his backpack and poured out the contents, focusing on the head and hands. Holy water, used, just as we'd been instructed, to speed up the decomposition and prevent the identification of the remains if the cops arrived before it dissolved into sludge. Almost invisible blue flames sprang up, and the smell of rotten flesh being cooked assaulted me. Coughing, trying not to retch, I took several steps back and scanned the area. After a few deep breaths, my stomach settled and Brother Malachi put away the canteen and swung his gear back on. He wiggled a bit and his backpack was settled comfortably.

"Fight's over," he said. "Come on, we might be needed for cleanup." We headed back up the hill.

"Okay," I said, following him. "What were those bird things? Some kind of harpy?"

"Hell's Valkyries. Tough to summon, tough to control, so my guess is one of the witches was a necromancer, and a powerful one. Normally, they collect the willing souls for Hell when someone dies. The unwilling souls are taken by ghasts. They look like a purple-black shadow. Thin, like a ribbon, kinda man-shaped. If you ever see one, run. I don't know of anyone who's stopped one."

"What's a ghast, and why don't I know about these things?" I felt like the slow child in class, laughed at behind his back. My misery must've shown, because when he looked back at me, Brother Malachi stopped.

He scanned around us for a long moment then turned to me. "Sebastian, how many different types of beetle do you think there are in the world?"

I shrugged.

"There are over one hundred thousand. No one, not even the best entomologists, know every type. They know the common ones, or the ones in their area, or the ones they study. When they see a new kind, they ask someone else or refer to a manual. What makes you think there are fewer minions and creatures of Hell than types of beetle?"

"Oh," I said, now feeling foolish for being petulant.

"Don't worry. In a few more years, you'll be answering the questions, not asking them. You've only been doing this a couple of years. No one expects you to be an expert yet."

I looked down to hide the burning flush on my face. I'd been acting childishly.

"And remember, you've seen more than any of your classmates. Not read about it or seen a picture on a screen, but encountered it in real life. Don't be in a hurry to see more. You'll live longer."

When I looked up, he had a small smile on his face. I took it as a sign of kindness rather than mocking.

"You're right," I said, trying to accept my ignorance, though it still hurt, just a bit. I was used to being the smartest kid in class, and having to ask questions all the time rankled.

Brother Malachi waited a moment, giving me time to grow up, I guess, before turning back up the hill. "We'd better check in."

We went to rejoin the others.

CHAPTER 21

Interlude—The Body

As the sun rose in the sky and the temperature climbed, the house creaked in an almost satisfied way. The faint tang of blood sacrifice hung in the air, overlaid with the smell of magic—sweet to some, revolting to others. Down in the subbasement, where it was perpetually chilly and blood misted the air, final preparations were at hand. It was almost over. As always, of course, there were surprises for the unwary.

The sacrifices were chosen not only for their lack of connection to the mundane world, but also for their health and physical appearance. There were five men and three women, as prescribed by the ritual. All under twenty-five, they had piercings and tattoos to demonstrate their "independence." They also all wore the slack expressions of cattle just before slaughter, empty husks devoid of personality, yet they stood upright, walked, and responded to verbal commands. Their eyes, the filmy look of the dead, gave away their true condition, but the rest of their body hadn't quite caught on, yet. Despite the eight sacrifices, the three necromancers, and their protection, the room seemed only half full, as though it grew to accommodate each new arrival.

With no electricity in the house, severed heads of kittens stapled to chains and then set alight had been affixed to the ceiling. The heads, still alive, yowled faintly as they burned a sickly yellow-green and provided illumination. Muscle dragged boxes containing supplies and instruments of power down to the sub-basement. With each step, dust, somehow sticky and smelling of the graveyard, puffed up and coated everything. A sideburn-wearing warlock, his facial hair glistening in the light, led the preparations, assisted by a taller, cadaverous man who appeared too old to be alive. Gray tufts of hair just above his ears were all that remained on his liver-spotted skull. The last necromancer, a short, fleshy man bedecked with rings, moved nimbly despite his bulk.

"There are protective wards there, there, and there," said the leader, pointing to thin ribbons of dirty red light, which rippled as though something swam just under their surface. "Nick," he said, turning to the tall necromancer, "check the tomes."

Nick nodded once. "Yes, Eric." He crossed the room to one of the large boxes, opened it, and pulled books out of a crate. Some of them moved on their own and snapped at each other and at him. He shuffled through the books until he came to a small, slim volume bound in pale green pockmarked skin. Nick whispered a word of power, and it opened in his hands. Light came from the pages and bathed his sweating face as he read.

"Phil," said Eric to the fat necromancer. "The wards. I want you to consult with the departed. Jane is your best bet, I think."

Phil silently slid over to a Muscle holding a box as though presenting it to someone. Shapes that seemed to be a parody of the human form writhed and moved on the box, and Phil opened the front to reveal three severed heads, each resting on and held in place by a dirty-yellow crystal collar. Two were male, the middle one female. The eyes were open and aware. Phil chanted, and the heads smiled in anticipation. When Phil was done, Jane spoke in a voice that was a combination of old woman and heavy smoker.

"Show me," she commanded, and Phil stepped out of the way so the head could survey the room.

"Clever," she said as the head rotated, looking at the wards. "Well built, but easy enough to remove."

"Tell me," grunted Phil, and Jane gave him instructions.

Eric took off his shirt to reveal a well-muscled chest. He spoke a word and drew a circle on his chest with a finger. The flesh stretched outward, pushed forward by a misshapen head the size of a baby's.

The head twisted and turned until it was looking up at Eric then said in a sibilant whisper, "What do you wish, my master?"

"Do they suspect?"

The head stretched out further, and looked at the other two necromancers one by one. "No, but they are wary."

"Good. Tell me how to reassemble the body."

Nick finished and set the tome down on top of a chest, wiping sweat away. He looked over at Eric, who was quietly communicating with his imp, and then shared a nod with Phil. Eric was necessary only for so long. Eric placed a hand on the imp's head and shoved it slowly back into his chest.

Following Jane's instructions, Phil defeated the wards—their snapping, crackling energies winking out of existence. Next he pulled out a clear crystal rod and ball of thin copper wire. He wrapped the crystal seven times with one end of the wire and tossed the remainder across the intricate patterns carved into the floor. A series of small bolts of electricity snapped up from the floor, moving and twisting as though aware, and the rod flared an orangey-green color.

"Clear," Phil told the others when the glow faded.

Phil turned to two of the Muscle, "You two," he commanded, pointing at each one in turn. "Working from the outside in, empty the boxes and gently remove the contents. Put the boxes in the corner over there," and he pointed to a mostly clear spot.

Two set of vacant eyes tracked his finger to the spot indicated, and then the Muscle swiftly emptied the chests. Inside each were human remains, which they placed reverently on the ground. The last chest held a torso, and when they moved it, they revealed a dark oily spot the size of a manhole cover that contained a small puddle of liquid, like oil but far darker. Bits of flesh and excrement floated on the surface, and the fluid swirled. Purple-black power, another ward previously unseen and unexpected, formed a ring around the puddle and surged up to the ceiling. The puddle stirred and moved as a figure rose from its depths as though on an elevator.

A triangular head, shaped like a praying mantis's with massive protuberant eyes and ragged pointy ears at the top two corners, emerged first. As the oil-like substance flowed away, the creature's true color, a dark red, was revealed. It laughed, its mandibles clacking together, at the three magi who'd taken an involuntary step back when they recognized what it was.

"A grendle," said Phil as the creature continued to rise. Its torso was humanoid, massively muscled, and hairless. Two ragged bat-like wings sprouted from the middle of its back. The wings spread slightly and shook off the oil.

"A crude term," it said in a soft, beatific voice, looking around at the room and its occupants, "but acceptable for now."

A chain around the grendle's neck sizzled and burned where it made contact with the flesh of its chest, raising pink welts that faded almost as quickly as they were made. The pendant on the chain was a head in a cage, made of silver and meteoric iron, which gleamed dully in the light. The eyes of the head were open and aware. An evil smile appeared on its lips, and the mouth opened as though to speak, but no sound came out.

The grendle finished rising out of the oily substance. It had no visible genitalia and its legs were red and insect-like, with a serrated ridge down the front of the lower leg below the knee joint, ending in the small dainty feet of a girl. It lifted a hand toward the ward, reaching out with three long, claw-tipped fingers. The vapors became solid and the grendle snatched its fingers back as though burned.

"Disturbingly effective," it said sadly. "Free me, and I shall reward you beyond your dreams."

"No," said Eric, shaking his head. "We're here to bring Thaddeus back."

The grendle cocked its head at an unnatural angle and gazed unblinkingly at the warlock for a moment. "What is your name, magi?" The voice, still soft, took on a compelling tone.

Eric shook his head. "Give you control over me? No. Either you know my name or do not, but I will not speak it here and now."

"It will be difficult to teach you, to educate you, to share my secrets with you, if I do not know your name and share mine. A bargain many would kill for."

"We're not here to learn from you, but to release Thaddeus."

The creature paused for a moment, seemingly weighing options, making plans. "I do nothing for free, little magi."

"We do have a small gift for you, to repay you for your service to Thaddeus, if you accept our offer."

The grendle stopped moving, held absolutely still. Then, slowly, nictitating membranes slid across its eyes. The membranes closed, and there was a brief pause before they opened again. "Make your offer," it said calmly, "but if it is insulting, you will pay." The last phrase echoed through the room, causing Phil, the fat necromancer, to take another step back.

"We have eight captive souls for you, willingly given."

The creature stopped moving again. A parody of a smile crept across it face, and it snaked a long pink tongue out to lick a mandible.

"Oh, little magi, you do know how to bargain," it said. "What are your terms?"

"You depart this realm, harming no one present including Thaddeus. If possible, for the next three earthly hours, you will protect us from any demonic, churchly, or magical attacks, either impending or within one mile of this location. If not, you will warn us as quickly and clearly as possible. Additionally, you can't inform any sentience of what's occurred here until one earthly day after Thaddeus is reborn."

"Well said," it replied. "I do like clever. Are you sure you're not a lawyer?"

"When I sell my soul, it will be for more than a not guilty verdict."

The creature gave off a chittering laugh. "Thaddeus and I have had many conversations while we've been here, traded many stories and ideas, among other things. I will be sorry to see him go. Fair warning, you'll find him to be very different."

"Do you accept?" asked Eric.

"What of the one who did this?"

"Thaddeus will want his vengeance. I'm sure you'll approve of what will happen to the upstart apostate. As additional recompense for your patience in this matter, you may have the servant who brings you the souls."

The creature laughed again. "Thaddeus and I have spoken at length on the subject of revenge. It does occupy his mind at times. Almost compulsively, it seems. No matter. I have made a few suggestions, and I have been promised a viewing when it occurs." It smiled and opened its arms as wide as it could. "I accept your offer."

The necromancers quickly dispelled the last ward and freed the grendle, who remained in the same spot, observing them.

Eric pointed at one of the Muscle. "Get the box of souls and give it to the grendle."

The Muscle turned and went to a pile of equipment. He picked up a large chest made of clear crystal with golden accents and handles, with a swirling whitish mist inside. Faces in horrific agony pressed against the sides, trying to escape. The Muscle walked across the room, watched by all, and presented the chest to the grendle.

The creature took the box with one hand and, with an unnatural gentleness, touched the Muscle with a single digit. The Muscle shuddered and his skin transformed into gray-black ash under the grendle's finger. The spot grew in size, rushing up the arm, turning the skin the color of burned paper. The Muscle moaned, and his torso was engulfed. As the mutation washed over his face, he tried to scream, but all that came out was a puff of ash. Everything was still when it was over, even the flaming undead kitten heads stopped their yowling, almost as though the world held its breath, waiting to see what would happen next. The grendle admired his handiwork for a short minute, his head once again tilted to the side. The moment over, the creature took off the necklace, Thaddeus's head bouncing inside, and smacked it into the remains of the Muscle, which broke apart and scattered. The grendle dropped the necklace on the hard dirt floor.

"Farewell, little magi," it said and faded away.

CHAPTER 22

There was a brief pause then the necromancers got back to work. Eric put on gloves to prevent burns then freed the head from its prison. He held it tenderly, cupping it under the neck so it could see around the room. Thaddeus's head smiled evilly, his eyes searching, roaming, and taking in all the preparations and activity. Eric rotated the head so he could look at Thaddeus's face, and they made eye contact. After a brief moment, the necromancer nodded.

On a blue tarp spread out on the floor, they piled the parts of Thaddeus together into a rough anatomical shape. Nick retrieved the tome he'd consulted earlier and led the chants. Phil developed a nose bleed, which he ignored, and Nick spat out a tooth. The body began to glow purple-black. Thaddeus's eyes rolled back into his head and his mouth opened in a silent scream. The glow pulsed and increased in intensity until the whole room was illuminated. When the light reached a constant brightness, the first sacrifice was summoned and given a knife made of sharpened crystal.

Nude, he knelt on the tarp next to Thaddeus's remains and swayed for a moment, chanting. When the chant ended, the sacrifice thrust the knife upward, under his ribs and into his liver. He twisted the knife and pulled it back out. He made no sound, but a sheen of sweat sprang up all over his body. Black blood gushed out of the wound, spraying onto the tarp and body. The blood sank into the gray skin, and the ragged ends of the body parts twitched and melted as though transformed into a liquid. Ooze from one of the thighs flowed until it touched the torso, and the two pieces snapped together like magnets, giving off purple-black sparks. The skin glowed where the parts reattached and solidified.

Next, strange shapes and sigils rose to the surface of Thaddeus's skin as though carved from the inside, and flashed the red of rusted steel. The necromancers stared at them, transfixed. Symbols soon covered every inch of the dismembered pieces, the shapes writhing as though alive and hungry.

They weren't any recognizable language or shape, but if one concentrated, they almost started to make sense. The effort hurt, though, like an icy dental pick digging into the brain, trying to free a memory.

Eric shook his head and stopped focusing on any individual sigil. He glanced over at the other two, who were still transfixed, and shoved Nick and then Phil to snap them out of their enthrallment. The sacrifice's body, now completely drained, had turned into a dried husk, curled into a fetal position. It looked like a mummy dug up from some desert. The eyes were gone, the lips and skin shrunk until the face seemed to sneer, and every bone clearly visible through the paper-thin, now nearly-transparent skin. The hair had changed from dark brown to brittle dirty white, ready to snap off at the lightest touch. Nick tried to kick the desiccated carcass aside as the next sacrifice approached, but it burst apart in a puff of dried flesh, large chunks flying everywhere then exploding into smaller pieces and more dust. Phil let out a cruel laugh as Nick spluttered, spitting skin from his mouth. Nick glared at Phil then reached into the dust and handed the next sacrifice the crystal knife.

By the fifth sacrifice, the body on the tarp was almost whole. The skin became a waxy yellowish color with the sigils continuing to swirl and pulse red, seemingly in time with a slow heartbeat.

When the last sacrifice died, Thaddeus let out a scream as loud as a jet engine, making the necromancers flinch. The scream echoed unnaturally around the room for several moments until fading out.

"Very good, my children," Thaddeus said as he stood. He looked down at his arm, where his left hand should've been, raising it to stare at the stump. The wound was open, as though the hand had just been removed, but it didn't bleed. "The slave was clever, and shall be repaid for this," he said, still staring at the missing part.

The necromancers stood in their row, awed by what they'd seen.

He slowly gazed at each of them in turn, a predatory look crossing his face. "First, I need magical replenishment. Eric, you know what to do," Thaddeus said to the leader, who was standing in the middle of the row.

Eric nodded, and two ethereal arms sprang from his back, each holding a knife. He plunged them into the backs of the other two necromancers and twisted. Surprise and shock formed on their faces as they arched up on their toes. A flowing ribbon of purple-black sprang from their chests and rushed across the space to Thaddeus, who opened his mouth and consumed the magic. Eric withdrew the knives—the two necromancers sank to the ground—and the ethereal arms and knives faded back into nothingness.

"Well done, Eric," said Thaddeus as the weaselly necromancer knelt in supplication. "Now, time for a new arm." He looked at the two dead necromancers and checked their arms. Evidently satisfied, he said, "This one will do."

Thaddeus's mouth stretched into a snout, and he bit through the arm with a single snap of his serrated teeth. He held it to his stump and spoke words of power as his face reformed into a more human shape. Snake-like tendrils of yellow and red flesh oozed from his forearm, bridging the gap between his stump and the new hand. With a sizzle, his skin fused to the stolen flesh as though the different skins were welding together. More tendrils surged out of his forearm until the skin arched the gap completely. With a *snap*, bones fused. After waiting a few more seconds, Thaddeus turned the hand over and flexed the fingers one by one. The white hand was smaller than his other, but Thaddeus seemed pleased.

"Very nice indeed," he said with a smile that had nothing to do with happiness. Thaddeus turned to the still-kneeling Eric. "Come. We must prepare before we search for the apostate. Then we can offer him chastisement."

"Master," asked Eric as he stood up, "we're not going after him first?"

"No," he replied, "others will have heard of my rebirth. Some will be returning to me to be of help. Others, thinking I'm bereft of power, will be here to try to steal. We must welcome both. I also have an interesting entity you should meet."

"Master?" said Eric, looking perplexed.

Thaddeus leaned into Eric and placed an arm around the necromancer's shoulders, managing to make the gesture at once friendly and menacing. Eric didn't cringe but his face grew white.

"Tell me, Eric," said Thaddeus, "what do you know of wood sprites?"

CHAPTER 23

Sebastian

We regrouped with our teammates in the little valley where the battle had taken place. As we made our way downhill and approached the rest of the team, I looked around to see what had occurred and, morbidly, if we'd lost anyone. Sadly, a body bag was being loaded into a waiting SUV, not far from the few others who were getting bandaged. I didn't hear screams or moans or see any frenetic activity, and figured we'd come through this fight mostly unscathed. I let out the breath I hadn't even realized I'd been holding.

We got lucky, I thought. *Wonder how long that'll last?*

I shook my head to drive the thoughts away. I needed to stay focused—I couldn't afford to let the others down, or look weak. The electronic clock buzzed, and almost by habit, I looked over my shoulder at the empty desert we'd left behind. Once back on the road, I stopped for a second, watching. Clean up was progressing rapidly. Several Hammers were stomping on smoldering piles of grass. Over to my left, a line of Hammers advanced along the road, picking up brass, dropped magazines, and other hard-to-explain items. A good fifty feet in front of them, like some bizarre band leader, was a Hammer wearing old-fashioned brass goggles. On his back was an enormous spray pumper that could've been from Sherlock Holmes's time. He moved slowly, as if each step were an effort. Jets of water streamed out of the nozzle in his hands, hitting burning bits of debris, body parts, and other, less normal, items. Sometimes the flames went out, other times it was as though he were spraying gas. When the stream hit a collection of lich body parts, purple-black flames shot up and the pieces melted away.

Brother Malachi, realizing I'd stopped, turned back to me. Giving a wave in the direction of the steampunk Hammer, he said, "The tank's got holy water in it. Puts out some fires, burns other things up."

"Damn, that's clever," I said. "Why didn't we do that in New England?"

"Regular Inquisitors fight skirmishes—one witch, one team. Hammers fight wars—lots of witches, lots of teams. More mess, less time for cleanup. They gotta get creative."

"Huh." I got moving again.

Brother Malachi walked next to me, still talking. "I know you think of these guys as simple, just here to tear stuff up, and that's true to an extent, but they also have to think. The enemy is more powerful than we are, so brute strength alone will fail unless someone knows how to use it, where to hit, and when. And, unlike witches, we care about riling up the police." Without looking at me, he raised an arm in front my chest, stopping me mid-stride. "You stay here. I'm going to find out what's next. Maybe offer a suggestion or two."

I didn't say anything as the action was kind of rude, and took me by surprise.

Brother Malachi clomped off, and I looked about to see if there was something I could do besides stand in the middle of the road. Brother Seth, along with a few others who seemed to be in charge, were standing around the hood of one vehicle, talking in low tones.

"All right then, little Brother," said one of the Hammers as he strode over to me. It might've been a question or a greeting. I still wasn't great with accents, thanks to Thaddeus mucking about in my brain, but his cadence made me think he wasn't an American. Another of the large variety of Hammers, he was at least six and a half feet tall, wide as a door, with a flat, freckled, open face, and short brown hair. He put out his hand to shake.

"Brother Tristan from old Blighty here to learn a few things before I help sort out our own problems back home."

I took the proffered hand, which enveloped my own, and shook it. There was a lot of controlled strength in that hand, but the grip was only firm, not crushing.

"I'm Brother Sebastian." Part of what he'd said seemed odd to me, but first I wanted to know who was in the body bag. "Do you know who didn't make it?"

"Brother Austin. Did you know him?"

"Not really. He was always on a different team. White guy, big like you. Had sandy blond hair."

"That was him. I worked with him on a mission once. Nice. Quiet. Think he came from Oregon." He lowered his eyes and clasped his hands together at his waist. "God comfort him."

"Amen," I responded automatically, crossing myself. He stood there, silent for a moment, and then I remembered the strange phrase he'd used. "Old Blighty?"

His mood changed rapidly, the serious frown replaced by a smile. "England, you silly colonist." His smile grew wider and his brown eyes were lit up with merriment.

His humor was juvenile, and infectious, and what I needed after the stress of combat and loss. Unlike some, I didn't get the shakes as the adrenaline wore off, but I did tend to get melancholy and wrapped up in myself. Talking helped me avoid that, and humor was always appreciated.

"Colonist?" I retorted, getting in on his act. "Last I checked, we beat old King George and started our own country."

"True," he said, with a sad smile, "but I'm sure if you ask really nicely, we'll let you back in."

"And why would we want that?"

"So we can teach you how to make bloody fish and chips properly." He gave a deep, rumbling belly laugh. I had to smile. "Listen, we're about done here, and I have a ripping good idea I want to share. You game?"

"Okayyy," I said. "Do you think we have time?"

"Brother Manuel there," he said waving to the group of leaders, "is our team leader. He says we have both ends of the road blocked and the police won't be here for hours, if they come at all. I mean, we're in the bloody desert, right?"

"All right. What's this idea of yours?"

"Now, I'm a city boy, but I've always wanted to be a cowboy. Ride a horse, chase some cows, learn to saunter, maybe even chew tobacco. I figure there's gotta be others in England who want the same thing. So what I'll do is buy up some farms in Cornwall, and set up a dude ranch."

The man's lost it. I tried for a straight face. "A dude ranch," I said, "in England."

"Sure," he continued. "I'll call myself Bucky. That's a good cowboy name. My ranch will be the Rocking B. I can hire some birds, put them in gingham, whatever the hell that is, and we can have hoedowns on Saturdays. I'll feed them all beans and beef. Can you see some stuffy banker down from London, walking about in jeans, learning to sing to the doggies and keeping an eye out for rustlers?"

I could, and it was ridiculous. "Umm," I said, my eyes watering as I fought my laughter.

Brother Tristan kept going, ignoring my facial contortions.

"It'll be brilliant. I'll be a billionaire in no time, hanging out with Richard Branson. I may even get a knighthood out of it."

"Sir Bucky?" I gasped and let loose.

He stood there for a moment, staring at me, then joined in. It felt good just to laugh and enjoy his absurd idea.

"I always need a laugh after...after something like this. Keeps me from getting the shakes," said Tristan, He wiped his eyes, and his face got serious. "So tell me, how did you end up in this life?"

For us, it was a normal question. We lead a strange life, and it's always good to get an affirmation that you're not the only one. I gave him the quick, less painful version. "I was a research chemist. I liked to buy old alchemy books to see if they held any ideas I could use. Last book I bought was a grimoire. A witch wanted it, so she sent a minion to collect. It killed my wife and dog, set fire to the house. I was blamed. Sent to a mental hospital for observation. The Brethren sprung me, and I've been a monk ever since."

"Hard transition?" he asked.

I looked down at the ground, my heart twisting. "I miss her every day."

"Oh. Shite, man." I looked up at him quickly. His face had a hound dog look of sorrow on it. "Sorry. I meant going from science to...to this," he said with a wave of his arm.

"Oh, umm," I muttered as it took me a second to switch mental gears. "I had a lot more initial doubts than the other novices, but it's tough to argue with observable phenomena."

He chortled. "True. I like the way you phrased it. Observable phenomena."

"And yourself? How did a cowboy from England end up in Arizona?"

He gave me another broad smile. "Let me tell you how a young hooligan became a monk."

Brother Tristan had been born in Yorkshire in a council flat, which, he explained, was subsidized housing in England. His parents rarely held a job, preferring to smoke, drink, and watch television. "Not bad people, really," he said, "just ones who preferred not to work for a living."

Despite their poverty, his parents were married and stayed together, unlike most of his friends' parents. He and his siblings had little parental guidance, and did as they pleased.

"We were a right bunch of savages, mucking about in old factories, breaking windows. The usual juvie stuff. Surprised we never got caught, but I guess we always ran faster than the others, so my parents never got visits from the police or the council."

The only exception to this freedom was Mass on Sundays. "We could expect a proper thrashing if we missed," he said.

He was ten when he saw his first witch, and reacted like most.

"I hid in my room for the rest of the week. Me mum had to wallop me to get me to go to Mass. I asked one of the Sisters who taught Sunday school if there were demon people, because I'd seen one. She didn't believe me at first, so I described the witch in detail. Word got around, and a few days later, we received a visit from a monk. He was waiting for me when I got back from school. We went into my room, and after some coaxing, I told him what I'd seen and that I was scared. He told me not to worry, that they'd protect me and my family, but I'd have to come to a new school, live there during the school year. I agreed. We went back into the living room, and he told me mum that I'd been offered a scholarship to attend Catholic School. She was chuffed. They gave me a fine education, and when I graduated, I became an Inquisitor. We have to be even more low-key than you colonists, so we do our training here."

"A lot of witch problems in England?" I asked.

"Bit of a mess, really," he said. "We're not the old battlegrounds, like the Continent and Middle East, but we did invent Wicca. Some of those fools get sucked in way deeper than they ever meant to. There's some real blindness to certain activities under England's desire to be 'tolerant.' You know, refusing to judge the behavior of minority groups to be inclusive and understanding. People trying to be cool and risqué get sucked into evil, and we have to deal with the results, if we can. But the really dangerous ones are old money families who've mucked about with magic for generations."

"You have families involved in…in this?" I said, jerking my head at the rapidly disappearing battlefield.

He nodded with a serious frown. "More than a few, I'm told. Money and the deep British desire to avoid scandal can hide a lot of secrets." He punched one fist into the other hand to make his point. "Not everyone in the family is corrupted, but every generation has its witches and warlocks ready to burn the place down for more power." He shook his head sadly as he continued. "We have descendants of Victorian adventurers who saw something they shouldn't have, or engaged in rituals. I think they came back tainted and passed that along to their children, amongst other things. There are a lot of old tomes sitting around in private libraries that should've been Purged. Someone of a tainted bloodline innocently picks up the wrong book on a dreary Sunday, and a new monstrosity is born." He let out a sigh, and we stared at the ground.

"Ever been to the Vatican?" he asked. It took me a second to work out what he'd said.

"Um, no. I'd like to, of course."

"Went there just before I came here for training. Well worth the visit. Sublime, serene."

I liked the idea of going to Rome, of seeing the Vatican and maybe getting away from everything for a bit. I was mulling over the idea and what I'd like to do there when Brother Malachi returned, glanced at Brother Tristan, and said to me, "Sebastian, the SUVs are coming here. We need to load up. I'll get you up to speed once we're on the road."

"Is the wee one with you then, Brother Malachi?" asked Brother Tristan, turning toward him.

"Yes," replied Brother Malachi. "But I wouldn't call him 'wee.' If he took offense, you'd have a stay in the hospital to regret your word choice."

There was a moment of uncomfortable silence as Brother Tristan digested this while his eyes darted between myself and Brother Malachi.

"Oh well, if he's one of yours, I understand. As the Bard said, 'he's small but fierce.'"

"Quite right," said Brother Malachi. "I wouldn't have been able to handle that construct without him."

Brother Tristan let out a long whistle and turned back to me. He was no longer smiling but looking intently at me. "Just the two of you?"

"Mostly Sebastian," said Brother Malachi.

"Impressive," said Brother Tristan, and offered me his hand again.

As we shook, the SUVs arrived. With a wave, Brother Tristan loped off to the first one.

Brother Malachi waited until he was a few steps away then said to me, "You need to be careful. You're new, and the other Hammers will try to establish dominance. It's a pack mentality with some juvenile hazing thrown in. If you let them denigrate you in any way, they'll lose respect for you. Then," he paused for a moment to make his point, "you will have to send one of them to the hospital."

"Hazing?" I asked. "It didn't seem that way to me."

"You're thinking of frat house antics. This is more subtle. Little digs and putdowns. Just to see what you'll do."

I closed my eyes, turning my head a bit, contemplating his idea for a second. I was never big on status, and really didn't worry about where I fit, letting my actions speak for me. "Aren't you being unfair to Brother Tristan?"

Brother Malachi frowned and leaned in. "Perhaps. But, look, in any hierarchy, there are two pecking orders, the formal and informal. The best leaders are the ones who're respected for their ability as well as their position. The hazing is just a way to see what you will and will not tolerate and how you react. Think of it as a juvenile leadership test."

I nodded, but I still wasn't ready to make his leap from action to intent. "Okay, but what does that have to do with me? I thought I wasn't going to be on the Hammer teams. I thought I was with you."

"True, but you still have to fit into their mindset to be able to work with them."

I flushed. What more do they want? I've done everything required of me. I've led teams. Hell, I have the ring and the nightmares to go with it. I opened my mouth to protest when Brother Malachi held up a hand to stop me.

"Yes, you've met the standards to be a Hammer, but that's the minimum required. What else have you done? In their minds, are you capable? Why should they trust their lives to you? Trust comes from respect and consistency. In order to respect you, they have to know what you've done and believe you can do it again. You have to become a bit of a legend."

My anger drained out of me. What he was suggesting was absurd.

"Legend?" I asked with a wry smile.

"Yes. What is legend but the tales of heroics? You've done that. You've fought the good fight, they just don't know it yet."

"So I need to brag?"

Brother Malachi barked out a laugh. "No," he said, "I'll be doing the bragging. You, my friend, just have to survive."

132

I did want to be a legend. I wanted to show everyone who'd doubted me that they were wrong. A smile crept up on my face. "That sounds like an excellent plan to me."

"Good, now let's go show everyone what you can do."

With that, he led me off to our waiting SUV.

CHAPTER 24

After clearing our weapons and making sure the safeties were on, we climbed back into our SUV. We were convoying south to meet up with another Hammer team. Inside, we refilled empty magazines and rechecked our gear as we drove. Small plastic boxes containing our hand-loaded silver bullets were handed around. The *clack, clack, clack* of ammo being shoved into a magazine was oddly comforting. I was surprised to find I'd used up five magazines of ammo—almost a hundred and fifty rounds—and I was loading ammo long after everyone else had switched to checking on other gear. Impressive, in a way, but it shouldn't have taken me so many rounds. My marksmanship needed work.

When I finally finished loading my ammo, it was quiet, with none of the banter I was used to with regular Inquisitors. One Hammer was mending a tear in his combat vest. Others were resting or looking at maps. Brother Seth, in the front passenger seat, was on his cellphone calling in a sit-rep, explaining what had happened and what supplies we might need, and trying to get updates on what was next. Another Hammer was rooting around in a team box, trying to find a battery for his radio. He had a spare, as we all did, but we always carried two as one was bound to fail at a critical moment.

"Two is one and one is none," was the Hammer motto for gear. Simplistic, but so very accurate. Brother Steve, one of my teammates, had forgotten his spare flashlight in an early practical. His flashlight died while he was in a darkened building on the outskirts of town. He had to open a padlock by touch alone, which took him five minutes longer than it should've, then almost impaled himself on some exposed rebar as he crept through a pitch black room. When he couldn't find the proper window to exit, he ended up finishing the problem late. The frowning Proctors had made him run the twelve mile trail twice for failing to properly prepare for a mission, and he had to repeat the exercise. And that was letting him off easy, by their standards.

I stared out the window for a minute before I realized the sun was starting to go down. Shadows were darkening and merging. The oppressive heat would be letting up soon, and it would even get cold if we were headed to the mountains or high desert. Wiggling around in my seat to get comfortable, I realized I felt...good. Even though I'd been without a full night's sleep in several days, I wasn't tired. I was excited and, for some reason, content.

Won't last, I thought darkly.

It took a lot of work, but I was able to smother the negative part of me most of the time. I still had the occasional dark thought, but compared to the dreams, that pessimistic voice was nothing. Besides, I knew I could do this. I had to do this. I was going to prove myself worthy.

Once Brother Malachi and I finished checking our equipment, he turned in the seat toward me.

"Okay, we still don't know why the witches are headed toward the southern part of the state, but we do know that's where they're going. We know something's drawn a lot of them there. And we're not the only ones who've made contact. There've been a few other firefights, and some witches have been killed. So far, other than Brother Austin, God rest his soul, no one else has died or even been badly injured. Other teams haven't been so blessed.

"We recovered a grimoire from the warlock, but he died in the firefight. The two witches managed to get away and are being hunted by some smaller teams. I doubt they'll get far. Either we'll find them or their own kind will. A couple of witches have been captured by other teams and are being Put to the Question to find out what's going on."

"Put to the Question" was a polite euphemism for torture. The act hurts us more than them. We stain our soul; they get some temporary pain. You can't really

135

hurt a witch with torture. Not permanently, anyway. They can regenerate, heal, very quickly, and they endured far more pain than we could ever dish out during their transformation into a witch. We could, however, take away their hope. They were brittle that way. Remove their belief that they can escape, convince them that their life is over, remove their power… that's what broke them. But even broken, they remained defiant, proud of what they'd done. All were offered a chance at redemption. All refused.

Part of me still recoiled at the thought of torture, but it was the only way to get information. It wasn't like we could turn them over to the cops. They'd be far more likely to arrest us once we told our story. And even if the witches were arrested, jail couldn't hold them—they'd just take over the place and walk out when they ran out of people to torment and sacrifice. Still, that we had to sink this low made my skin crawl. I did what I had to, and nothing further, but every time I Put a witch to the Question, I hated myself a little more.

Something must've shown on my face, because Brother Malachi stopped for a second and leaned in toward me. "I know. There's no other way, but I wish there were."

Several of my mentors over the years have said the same thing at one time or another, but far too many of my Brethren are of the 'just desserts' mentality. That cavalier attitude on such a corrupting issue worries me, even now. I still fear becoming blasé and inured, readily accepting the situational ethics, until one day I no longer recognize myself in the mirror.

Brother Seth turned back to us. "Update. They're headed to Durango. Still don't know why. We should be there in another hour or so."

CHAPTER 25

James

On the way to Durango, I learned more about Glaive and his metal spirit. We were connected by a kind of mental bond, and I could command him with my thoughts, though it would take time for him to understand anything more than simple instructions. As we communed, we drove through a few small towns and lonely gas stations, never stopping. Occasionally, a car would pass us going the other way, and once a police cruiser followed us for a few miles before turning off. Otherwise, the road was empty, and I could concentrate on learning more about my new servant.

Far too heavy and big for the passenger seat, Glaive sat in the back, hunched over, the cymbal hat touching the roof. The idea of having a servant pleased me, and one who was absolutely devoted and loyal made me smile. I knew the treachery of other kinds of servants, and wouldn't make the same mistake as Thaddeus. Glaive was mine and would be a valuable tool, with some work and patience. At the speed of thought, we progressed rapidly, although I did, on occasion, lapse into words, which slowed things down.

As we got closer to our destination, the sun finally set, and when the full moon rose, it seemed closer than normal, lighting up the road and desert. This was a wilder part of Arizona, one of the reasons Thaddeus had traveled here—few people, lots of empty, open space, and old, forgotten entities to summon and learn from. The earlier fields or the odd herd of cows had given way to plain desert stretching far off into the horizon, only broken by the occasional mesas, rock clumps, and the lonely cluster of cacti twisting into semi-human shapes. It was almost as though they were designed to confuse. The thought of sentient vegetation, working to befuddle and trap prey, made me smile.

As I understood more, I realized that Glaive was good for simple tasks, but the spirit was the true intelligence. Kind of like a cerebrum and cerebellum. Glaive handled the routine, and the spirit did the thinking. The original spirits were there at creation. This was one of thier more recent offspring, a mere two hundred and fifty years old. The spirit had a name, but it was the sound of metal being cleaved, unpronounceable to me. I thought about calling it Bob, but eventually decided on Steel. While old and wise in the ways of metals, Steel didn't have a soul or understand human concepts like right and wrong, or cause and effect, or deceit. Normally Steel would've been deep in the earth, where heat and pressure form bizarre and exotic metals. These metals would be studied, and sometimes copied or shaped into objects and patterns that pleased the spirits. They had little contact with humans, and that was just fine with them. Roberto had tricked Steel into our realm with an offering of metalized sodium with a unique crystalline structure. Like all sentient beings, Steel hated being captive, and sought release, but as long as Glaive existed, Steel was bound to Glaive and compelled to do my bidding.

It offered me the usual panoply of treasures if I released it: riches, knowledge, and mates. Not human mates, mind you, but other spirits. Part of me couldn't help wondering how a spirit could take enough shape to consummate the relationship, but, realizing this was a diversion, I got back on topic. I'd thought about antagonizing it by demanding the impossible. Asking for its progenitor's name, or the world's supply of copper, but decided information was more important than the fun of tormenting a captive. There were holes in its understanding of our world, and I needed to fix those to make it a proper servant. Roberto had spent a lot of time training it to understand human concepts—like distance, time, weight, the periodic table—but there were still gaps.

"How far away can you detect meteoric iron?" I asked.

"What is meteoric iron?" it responded.

"Iron not originally of this earth."

"Five of your miles."

"What can you tell me about meteoric iron at that distance?"

"Size, purity, shape, depth under the ground, and many other facts, but wouldn't you rather have the gold in the ground nearby? I could give it to you in exchange for my freedom."

I didn't bother responding. I couldn't bribe my way out of Thaddeus's revenge.

"Do you have to touch metal to reform it?" I asked.

"No. I can do that at a distance. The softer the metal, the further away I can be."

I had visions of breaking into safes and banks as a hobby. I let myself have a mental grin then got back to finding out its capabilities.

"Can you heal Glaive if he lost an arm or leg?"

"I can rebuild every part of the creature, except its eyes and its heart."

That made sense. Glaive's eyes were a synthetic emerald, grown in Roberto's lab. Their vision was enhanced magically, and flickered as though on fire. His heart was the capacitor that powered him, buried deep in his chest and heavily protected. After the initial surge of electricity that had brought him to life, all he really needed was the bond to a magi to keep from reverting to an inanimate object. Electricity powered Glaive, but magic kept him alive.

I continued my questions, thinking of abilities that might come in handy. "Can you tell if an object that was formed into one piece has been altered?"

"Yes, but I must be much closer."

"Very well." If the reliquaries or the chains had been damaged, Steel should be able to detect it. Most likely, Thaddeus had escaped, perhaps with help, and become whole again, but there was always the possibility that he was still in pieces, and vulnerable.

"Master, another magic user approaches. They are eight miles away and closing rapidly," said Glaive.

Usually it's easy to spot one of the magi, but they have to be visible. Glaive was able to sense them from much further out. I again marveled at Roberto's cleverness. It was a shame I hadn't had the time to spare to heal and subdue him. He would've been useful.

"From what direction?"

"They are coming from the rear."

"Have they spotted us yet?"

"I don't know."

Continuing was a bad option. I was getting close to Durango. If they didn't know where I'd put the body, I'd just end up leading them there. Running would use up time I didn't have. Stopping gave me more options. I could bluff or fight or seem to flee across the desert. I pulled over on the bottom of a small hill and got ready. Glaive loped off into the darkness, following my instructions. Reaching out, I sensed an interesting presence and made contact. It took me only a few minutes to prepare and have a nice surprise waiting.

CHAPTER 26

I was ready by the time a van crested the hill. Lights from a house shone in the distance. If this turned noisy, I wouldn't be able to linger. I had no need of conies nor power to waste getting rid of the curious or police. Other than the house, the area was empty.

Good spot for an ambush, but if it comes to battle, you'd better be fast, I thought, looking back at the van.

It paused at the top of the hill for a moment then slowly eased down to where I leaned with my back against the car door. My weapons were ready but out of sight. I'd crossed my arms so that the severed hand wasn't visible. It would only take a word or two to activate if needed. The van stopped a bit behind my car, keeping me in its headlights, until they switched off. I tensed just a little as the side door opened.

She got out of the van and approached me. The way she moved made me think of a snake, all curves and sinuous motion. Lovely and deadly at the same time. She seemed bathed in light, her features in clear focus. Waist-length dark hair reflected the moonlight, and her lips were full and red. A pink tongue, thin but long, raked across her lips as she moved toward me, devouring me with large, backlit blue eyes, which were full of lust, and animal cunning. Her dress was tight and sheer, yet covered enough to make promises. I felt the urge to drop to my knees and please her in any way she asked. The severed hand twisted in mine, but I didn't pay attention. I was busy staring at the beauty gliding toward me.

"*It's her,*" Glaive said in my head, snapping me out of my fixation.

I was dealing with a sorceress, and a powerful one at that. Now, knowing the truth, I could see past the glamor to the real woman—still attractive, but not the goddess of female sexuality I'd seen before. I hardened my mind, forcing the more primitive part of me to be still.

I held up my free hand to stop her before she got within spitting distance. Coming in contact with her saliva could mean the end of my freedom. Now it was diplomacy time. There were forms to observe while each party figured out the pecking order.

Battles are more fun, I thought. *But, perhaps, you can find out something useful first.*

"I see you, Minerva, and I listen," I said, using the traditional greeting for a sorceress. Minerva was the Greek goddess of magic and wisdom, and sorceresses were nothing if not vain.

She let out a short musical laugh, full of humor and promise. It aroused me, and I hated her for her ability to get me to react.

I will never be a slave again, I vowed.

Part of me felt violated. I wanted to lash out, to rend her to pieces, to watch her beg for mercy that would never arrive.

Patience.

"And I see you, Mage." Her voice was sultry and had a hint of an accent, something dark and mysterious. It was the kind of voice one could listen to for hours and beg for just a few minutes more. Another beguilement. "If I may ask, what branch do you follow?"

"I know little, but I study all." I wasn't about to reveal my studies, as that would tell her my strengths and weaknesses.

"Oh, a polymath. I do love a smart man." She ran a hand along her side as though smoothing out a wrinkle. The fabric stretched and flattened, revealing more of her perfect body—one that needed to be held, ravished.

It would've worked had I not been warned and hardened my thoughts. Even with my preparations, I'd have to be careful—sorceresses have a lot of minions and can even enthrall creatures more powerful than themselves. I was done helping others; this was my time.

"I'm feeling a bit hungry. Would you care to join me for a light picnic?" Another trap; anything I accepted would incur debt on my part and would, most likely, be tainted. Sorceresses use cunning, guile, surprise, and ambush to win their battles. While not as strong as a battle mage, they're just as dangerous. Maybe more so.

"I'm happy to talk, and I thank you for the offer, generous as it is, but I cannot accept," I said.

"Pity. I was hoping for some dinner conversation, before I relax a little." Her emphasis hinted at hours of hot, sweaty sex. I could see her legs wrapped around my ass, gripping me, pulling me in deeper as I plunged into her and she cried out for more.

I forced the vision aside with a bit of mental effort. She was still trying, and I wasn't about to let her know she was wasting her time.

"A tempting, most gracious offer, but I must decline," I said, using the stilted language of formal, and overly polite, address.

"You refuse me?" she asked, arching one eyebrow, trying to bait me. Anger increases the power of a sorceress, makes her more dangerous, which is where the old saying, 'Hell hath no fury like a woman scorned,' comes from.

I had no desire to fight, not unless I knew I could win. For now, I needed to continue the dance of diplomacy.

"I refuse you nothing, Minerva, I merely decline."

A small pout formed, and she waited to see if it would work. We remained silent for a long moment. With a sigh, she let it go and asked, "What brings you out here?"

"I'm seeking wisdom."

She arched her eyebrow back up and even higher at this and her eyes bored into mine. "You wander? You have no home? You're feral? Should I take you in, keep you safe in my bosom?" she asked while cupping her breasts, the nipples hardened and jutted out through the fabric.

"I'm quite happy with my current demesne," I said, avoiding staring at her chest.

She dropped her hands, cupping them together at her waist and squeezing her breasts together with her biceps, making them plumper and arch out even more. Her nipples threatened to pierce the fabric of her dress. She held this pose for a long second and then said, "No, I think you should join me for my little adventure." She was getting persistent, dangerous.

The thrill of battle washed over me. I needed to change the subject before it became a demand, and left me out of options. "What adventure is that, Minerva?"

"I'm going to see Thaddeus and make him one of my pets. If you join me, you can have whatever's left. Baubles or minions I don't care for. I just want the man."

I felt the urge to laugh and almost smiled. She either had one hell of a plan or supreme confidence in her abilities to think she could enslave Thaddeus. "I thought he was dead."

"He was. He's come back, and I mean to make him mine."

Glaive reported to me via our mental link. *"I have located the men she dropped off. There are three and they have rifles."*

I had him describe the rifles, and it seemed she had some real snipers out there, or at least men equipped with a decent system. I understood her plan—if she couldn't convince me, or I attacked her, they'd open fire.

Clever girl. It would be a shame when she figured out her plans weren't nearly as good as mine. I focused on Glaive's thoughts.

"Can you eliminate all three at once?" I asked mentally.

"No, they are spread out. It will take me at least three minutes to remove them."

Very clever, I thought to myself.

She would be linked to all three, and unless Glaive could take them all out at the same time, she'd have the others kill me. Time for plan B.

I contacted Steel, and told him what I needed. He agreed, after some back and forth concerning his freedom, and Glaive set out on his new mission. The whole exchange had only taken a few seconds.

I refocused on the sorceress. "I'm intrigued by your proposal. Please tell me more."

"I had a necromancer in my stable. A few days before I found him, he'd been contacted by an associate and offered power if he could perform a resurrection. After a little bit of *persuasion*, he told me all. One of Thaddeus's disciples had been contacted, and knew of Thaddeus's location. Eric needed help, which is where Philip came in. I was intrigued and let him go, keeping only the smallest compulsion on him. He reported back that the ceremony was successful. Sadly, he was killed. Betrayed by Eric."

"The loss of a minion is always irritating," I said.

She gave a little shrug and curled her mouth down as though the loss was of no importance "Phillip was short, and fat. Not really suitable to be one of mine. His knowledge of necromancy was impressive, but he had few other skills." She changed the subject back to me. Her full lips spread in a wide entrancing smile. "What minions do you have? I don't see any in your car."

"Minions can be difficult," I said.

"Oh, I disagree." She shook her head slightly, causing her hair to ripple. "Yes, you have to bathe them and feed them, poor dears, and there's always some jealousy over who's most favored. But they can be so eager to please when handled properly."

"You sound as though you have talent in such matters."

"I have many talents. *Pleasurable* talents. You will know them all, if you join me."

"I'm still waiting to hear how you, formidable as you are, plan to subdue Thaddeus."

She made a little moue of distaste. "I don't tell my secrets to just anyone."

"I understand. I fear I've taken up too much of your time, and wish you success on your adventure."

The moue slid into a frown, and her eyes narrowed. "You will not refuse me on this," she said, stamping one of her feet, her seductive facade slipping.

"Again, I don't refuse, I decline."

Her face had changed into the look of a helpless maiden in need of assistance. I almost fell for it. "James," she cooed, trying once again to seduce. "You of all people know that Thaddeus must be stopped. When he's mine, I'll make sure he's occupied with other matters, and you will be free to do whatever your heart desires."

My hand twitched, ready to fight. I stopped moving, holding my breath. So she knew who I was and offered me safety in exchange for my help. It would come at a steep price, though. I would once again be a slave to another.

"Wise Minerva," I said, trying not to show how much it distressed me that she knew who I was, "I fear you do not know Thaddeus's power and will end up in his thrall. If I were to accompany you, my fate would be even less appealing."

"I insist," she said.

The time for diplomacy was over. I felt the internal smile, knowing I'd win yet another battle. I shook my head, and enraged her by saying, "No."

Her face contorted into a snarl, her hair billowed out as though windswept. She looked like an angel of death ready to claim another. She glowed the purple-black of magical power. "You will join me or die," she spat.

I gave her a smirk. "I think not."

The van doors opened and minions streamed out, only to be met by Glaive. Screams and the sounds of flesh being cleaved echoed off the nearby hills.

With a growl of fury, she unleashed a bolt of power at me, but I had a shield up and was already moving. Shots rang out from one side, but the bullets went nowhere. I'd had Steel warp the middle of the barrels. Just a little pinch. Not even noticeable to the naked eye. The explosion and gasses from the trapped bullets caused the gun to burst violently, flinging shrapnel like a long grenade.

Her bolt of power hit my shield with a wet *smack* and careened off into the night. Focused on me, she never saw my ally. The rock elemental I'd summoned earlier lurched into view. It was small, by their standards, perhaps eight feet tall, but safe and alone here in the desert. Perpetually grumpy, it took out its anger on the sorceress. One large hand lashed out at her and launched her into the air. She bounced across the road and landed in the dirt on the other side. I summoned up a binding, and long white tendrils wrapped around her until she was mummified and unable to move or speak. That done, I turned to the van, which was rocking. Wet, chopping sounds and faint screams came from within. I waited for Glaive to report that he needed help, or for the sounds to stop.

A few moments later, Glaive stepped out and walked over to me. He had quite a few dents and what looked like a scorch mark along one side. The swords were sheathed on his back, but he carried something in his hand.

"Are you okay?" I asked.

"I will require minimal healing," he said.

I glanced around and saw no cars, but the lights from the house were off. They could be headed out here to help. We had to finish this up quickly.

"Were there any magical items in the van?"

"Quite a few items with minor enchantments, and one grimoire, which I have retrieved." He held the book out to me.

I ran the severed hand over it. Other than the magic it contained, it held no traps.

"Open it for me," I instructed Glaive.

There's always a risk that too much knowledge will drive a person insane. It happens often to the cattle. Absorbing an entire grimoire in just a few seconds would warp anyone, which was why I had the hand do it for me, avoiding the problem. I spoke words of power, and an eye appeared on the palm of the hand. I commanded it to learn, and had Glaive turn the pages. It only took a few seconds before the hand had learned everything contained in the grimoire. I now knew all the secrets—the words of power, the ingredients for certain potions and enchantments and glamours—to being a powerful sorcerer. The ring glowed a dark purple for a moment as it drew power from the grimoire.

I had Glaive drop the grimoire and, with a word, set it ablaze. It screamed shrilly as the flames reduced it to ash. I thought about doing the same to the van, but figured a burning vehicle would attract even more attention than one full of chopped up bodies. It would take time for the police to react to the scene, and by then, I'd be long gone.

I turned to see the rock elemental standing over the sorceress. She was awake and struggling with the bindings, getting nowhere but managing to rock back and forth a little on the side of the road. She was why he'd agreed to help. He needed a mate.

Leaving Glaive and the burning grimoire, I walked over to the two of them.

"*Acceptable,*" it said to me mentally. It could hear well, but couldn't really form spoken words. "*A bit ugly, but I can fix that.*"

"*I'm sure she will provide you many fine offspring,*" I said. "*The binding will last until sunrise. Leave it on. She's powerful and will resist.*"

"*Only once,*" it responded, and there was a grinding of rock on rock that sounded like laughter.

I looked down at the sorceress, "Minerva, meet your new husband. I hope you'll be happy together."

Hatred blazed from her eyes and her mouth tried to move as though she were cursing me. All in vain; no sounds could escape the enchantment.

"Speak up, dear," I mocked, cupping a hand to my ear. "I can't hear you thank me."

The rock elemental bent down and picked her up. It stood and threw her over one shoulder.

"*Goodbye, mageling.*" It turned and strode back across the road and into the desert.

I drove off quickly, well pleased.

CHAPTER 27

Thaddeus and Eric were sitting on ornately fashioned chairs with a pitcher of lemonade sweating on a small table between them. The chairs were located on the sagging porch facing the road. Both men seemed to be waiting for something to arrive. Sounds of repair came from inside the house. Not hammers and saws, but the creaking and groaning of wood as it was reshaped.

"A house with its own wood sprite is quite handy," said Eric.

Thaddeus, who was holding a block of metal that he was caressing and crooning to, stopped for a moment and blinked. The block was both square and not at the same time, so black it seemed to draw light into it, and twisted and spun in his hands. He glared at Eric, who shrank back. With a flicker, Thaddeus's enraged face softened, and he gave Eric a sickly smile.

"I always reward those who are loyal, and know their place."

Eric began to stammer, and Thaddeus held up a hand to stop him. Eric's mouth snapped shut.

"To answer your question, the original owner of the house had a twisted wood sprite build it. When it was complete, he bound the sprite to the house for as long as it stood."

"How did you know, Master?"

"I learned much while I was... away. I had many conversations with the grendle. Some of the conversations were...disturbing, others illuminating."

Eric blanched at the thought of what would disturb Thaddeus.

"If not for my rage, I might not have come back or retained myself. I was offered many things, tempted beyond measure, but I remained whole."

A 1970's style station wagon appeared over the low hill in the distance, followed by a battered white pickup truck. Trailing a cloud of dust, the vehicles bounced and swerved, trying to miss the largest potholes. When they stopped in front of the house, Eric started to rise, but Thaddeus stopped him with a raised hand.

"Be still," he commanded.

Women, mostly tall and muscle-bound, piled out of vehicles, stretching and wiping dust from their faces. An enormous man-like creature, wearing an impossibly large suit but no shoes, rose from the bed of the pickup truck. The creature got out, the pickup swaying with each movement, and stood, arms crossed. Most of the women stayed with the vehicles, but one, short and wide, headed for the porch, sparing the man-thing a quick glance. She wore a leather vest over a flat chest and corpulent belly. A sleeve of tattoos covered each bare arm. Her hair was dyed blond and had been turned into a Mohawk, the sides shaved clean. Her pants were also leather and strained to hold her ample thighs. She walked to the first step of the porch and knelt, the leather pants creaking in protest.

"Master," she said, "I came as soon as I heard of your return."

"Judith, it is good to see you again," said Thaddeus. "Tell me why you were not here for my rebirth."

Judith looked up apprehensively. "Master...I didn't know. I didn't even know where you were when...when the incident occurred."

Thaddeus glanced over to Eric as she continued to stammer.

"It is as she says. I told no one of my find, and recruited the two fools from outside the coven," said Eric.

Thaddeus turned back to Judith. "Acceptable. What have you been doing while you awaited my return?"

Judith's face lit up with a smile. "Oh, Master, I believe I have a rare treat for you."

"Indeed?" said Thaddeus, arching one eyebrow imperiously at her. The challenge hung in the air for a long moment.

Judith, wisely, said nothing.

Thaddeus then made a show of looking at the nails of his white hand, comparing them to his other before saying, "Show me."

"Rook," she said over one shoulder, "bring it here."

The man-like creature went over to the station wagon and opened the rear compartment. He reached in and withdrew a dog carrier, which trailed a leash, clearly attached to whatever was inside. Eric leaned forward in his chair to get a glimpse of what was in the carrier, but could only make out a general shape. Thaddeus remained still, waiting for Judith to reveal her offer of renewed fealty.

Rook strode toward the front porch stairs then set the crate down a few feet away. Small hands, the size of an infant's but cruder and ending in claws, gripped the grill making up the door of the cage. A short hiss, low-pitched and cat-like, emanated from the cage.

All eyes turned to Thaddeus, who waved his hand and said, "Proceed."

Rook picked up the leash, opened the cage, and took a small step back. The creature inside strode out, head held high despite the manacles and collar. About two feet tall, he looked like the offspring of a human and a hairless demonic feline. The color of a bad sunburn, he had visible welts and bruises, showing he'd been mistreated recently. Small horns protruded from the smooth scalp. Yellowish eyes with oval pupils like a snake's glared up at the magi. Even the orbital sockets were ovals and canted at an angle. He wore a loincloth held in place by a belt that had pouches and straps for carrying tools and implements, now empty. He hissed again, showing a mouth full of sharp teeth and fangs. Silver clips gleamed in the sun and bound the creature's wings together, preventing flight. Smoke and the smell of burned flesh wafted up as the silver clips and manacles charred its flesh. Like Rook, the creature was unshod, but his feet had an opposable toe, able to grip objects, like an ape. There was a moment's silence as Eric and Thaddeus stared at the animal. Judith gazed up at Thaddeus, anticipation on her face. Rook looked out at the horizon, and the beast stared up at the sitting magi.

"Interesting catch, Judith," said Thaddeus. "But what do you propose I do with a homunculus I didn't create?"

"His progenitor is still alive, but in my care. If you're the closest mage when he dies, the connection will transfer to you."

Thaddeus shook his head sadly, and said with a snarl, "It doesn't work that way, you stupid bitch. If the progenitor dies, this creature will grow into his clone."

Judith flinched as though slapped. Her face went white, and she began to stammer again, "Master, I'm sorry...I didn't realize—"

Eric interrupted her. "Master, if we sever the connection, won't it reform to the nearest mage?"

"What do you propose?" said Thaddeus, turning toward Eric.

Judith stopped her waffling and listened attentively.

"A simple Faraday cage, made of silver. Put the creature in it, and the connection is severed. Open the cage back up and, if you're the closest, the homunculus becomes yours."

Thaddeus nodded, "Closer, Eric, but the creature must swear fealty in order to transfer to a new progenitor. He is sentient."

"He has no soul and therefore no free will, Master," said Eric.

Again Thaddeus glared at the necromancer, as his face morphed into a snout with long fangs gleaming in the sun. "Do not contradict me unless you wish to feel my wrath."

Eric quickly dropped his gaze and stammered, "Yes, Master. Of course."

Thaddeus quickly calmed down and even smiled a bit as his face deflated back into a human shape. "No harm, of course. This is a teaching moment." He waved his white hand at the creature below them. "He has the mirror of his progenitor's soul, so he has free will."

Eric, still staring down at the porch, said hesitantly, "Perhaps, Master, you could offer him a choice: duty or death?"

"And if he chooses death?"

Eric glanced back up at Thaddeus, seemingly surprised by the question, and didn't reply.

Thaddeus gave him a long, hard look then turned to Judith, who was also at a loss for words. He let out a sigh and said loudly, "Watch and learn, children." He stood up and looked down at the creature. Purple-black washed over him as he spoke a word of power.

"Creature," he said, his words filled with power and compulsion, "your progenitor will die. That cannot be changed. So you have but two options, fealty to me, or I'll have Judith blind and cripple you, torture you for days until you have no power left, and leave you in the desert for the animals to eat. The choice is yours."

The homunculus blinked a few times, turned to Judith, who was staring intently at him, and then back to Thaddeus. "My name is, and will remain, Top," he said in a deep bass rumble.

151

Thaddeus clapped his hands in school girl delight and said to Judith, "Oh, I like him. He's got spirit." Looking back down, Thaddeus said, "Acceptable."

Top sank to one knee.

Thaddeus waved off Rook, who dropped the leash and took several steps away. Thaddeus drew in more power, creating a ball of purple-black between his hands. He flung it over Top, where it morphed into a circle of power and settled on the ground, encircling the homunculus. Top mewled and lifted his head, pain clearly etched on his face.

Thaddeus glanced over at Judith. "Kill the progenitor."

Judith screwed her face up in concentration, sending a mental message. A long moment later, a black shape flitted along the ground and impacted the ward, shattering it into pieces. Two howls erupted, one from inside the ward and one from the pieces of the shape on the ground.

Thaddeus took several steps forward until he was almost touching the ward and dissolved it with a flick of his hand. A ribbon of black shot from the creature's chest and connected to Thaddeus. They were lifted off their feet by the enchantment, hovering inches above the ground. Thaddeus remained upright, while the creature twisted and writhed. The ribbon grew brighter, growing in intensity. Thaddeus's markings glowed red, and the same sigils and symbols were etched in a searing blue on Top, as though drawn from the inside. Both Thaddeus and Top screamed—Thaddeus in pleasure, Top in pain. The ribbon pulsed, pulsed again, and shattered, dropping both to the ground. Thaddeus landed lightly on his feet while Top collapsed in a heap.

Thaddeus wiped the sweat from his forehead and turned to Judith. "Heal him," he said, indicating Top with a hand.

Judith moved forward, a nimbus of purple-black appearing around one of her hands.

"Oh, Judith," said Thaddeus as he mounted the stairs, not looking back. "If you place a compulsion on him, I will take Rook away from you and punish you severely."

Judith nodded at this and quietly spoke words of power. The nimbus left her hand and covered the homunculus. Top writhed for a moment then sat up. The enchantment faded, and Judith quickly stepped back.

Top regained his feet. He turned toward Judith, hissed at her, and tensed, opening his wings as wide as the chains would allow.

"No," said Thaddeus, still walking away. "You will not attack any of my coven unless my life is in danger or I direct you to do so."

Top relaxed and gave a short nod. He looked back at Thaddeus. "The bindings, Master?"

"Judith," directed Thaddeus as he reached his chair.

Judith nodded at Rook, who walked over to Top, produced a key, and removed the restraints.

Top flexed his wings and launched himself into the air, fluttering over to the porch.

"Judith," said Thaddeus sitting back down. "Return his tools and introduce the rest of your coven to me."

CHAPTER 28

Sebastian

Brother Vincent disappeared when we stopped for gas. After that, things got worse.

We'd pulled into some nondescript mom-and-pop gas station as our SUV was getting a bit low. It also gave everyone a chance to stretch their legs, and use the bathroom. The station lights were weak and did little to ward off the darkness. As it was just a small gas station, it only had a single pump, so our SUVs were on each side of it, facing opposite directions. We put on our monk robes to cover the combat gear, and everyone was instructed to wear a placid expression to blend in.

I was press-ganged into being the food and drink fetcher. The guy running the station must've been in his eighties, and seemed peeved that we'd shown up.

"Almost closing time," he said to me when I walked through the door.

Very tanned, he had on a Stetson, and his eyes peered intently from the mass of wrinkles that was his face. A crooked, protuberant nose crested like the prow of an icebreaker. His bushy white mustache needed to be cleaned and combed. The flannel shirt he wore had at least a dozen stains, and his jeans, which I could just see over the top of the counter, were hitched up to below his sunken chest and held in place by a belt buckle that could've doubled as a butter dish

My God, I thought. *It's Yosemite Sam's dad. If he has a gun here, I bet it's an old Colt .45 Peacemaker.*

There was something about the man that made me want to laugh, or maybe it was the lack of sleep, or hysteria, or something. Whatever the case, the dark clouds that had followed me for the last few years seemed to vanish, for a while.

"We'll be quick," I said, thinking mellow thoughts lest I alarm him, and trying not to smirk.

"Whatta' you, some kinda monk?" he demanded with a frown.

"Yes, I'm one of the Poor Brothers." I kept an eye on him as I consulted the list and the selection in the coolers; some of the Brothers were not going to be pleased.

"Poor Brothers," the old man said, still glaring at me, with one hand below the counter, "is that some sort of cult?"

"No, we're Catholic, on our way to a retreat for some quiet meditation and prayer." The lie came easily but left an oily taste in my mouth.

"I'm Methodist myself," he said. "They call me Pops."

If this guy says 'rootin tootin,' I'm gonna lose it.

"I'm Brother Sebastian." I gathered the last of the drinks and brought them to the counter.

"Nice to meet ya."

I turned back and started to grab the snacks on my list as he rang up the drinks. The snack aisle seemed to run long on meats—jerked, pickled, and spiced—and short on carbohydrates.

No way I'm riding in a car with a bunch of guys eating that much protein.

I stopped for a second, thinking about what excuse I could use for not buying their snacks, when realized I was in front of a carousel of maps. An idea nagged me. I stayed there until it hit me that we needed more information and this guy might be a useful asset. I looked back at him. "Have you lived here long?"

"My whole life," said Pops, slowly examining each bottle before placing it in the sack. "Never understood why a grown man would drink something called Yoo-Hoo," he said, mostly to himself. It wasn't for me, so I wasn't offended.

"What do you know about Durango?"

"The old town or the new one?"

"There's more than one?"

"Old Durango was a mining and cow town. When the mine dried up, people moved, set up about fifty miles away. Old Durango was a bit up in the hills, close to the mine. Not much good pasture or farmin' up there. People moved to better

155

ground, easier access to roads, and kept the name. When the interstate came through, it was down here. Old place ceased to be a town about thirty years ago. Kids wouldn't stay, and the old folks died off. There's been talk of setting up some Old Western Town park with fake cowboys and shoot outs for the tourists there, but it never amounted to much."

Did The Brethren know there were two Durangos? Did it matter?

"So where is this old town? Might be worth seeing," I said.

"Not really much to see these days. There was a fire that burned down part. Kids and scavengers got most of the rest, excepting the old house, but you wouldn't want to see that."

"Why's that?"

"Creepy place," he said. "Folks said it was built by Old Granger, who was in league with the devil. They say you can still see lights there every now and then, but no one's lived there in years."

"Probably just kids," I said. *An old west haunted house? Sounds like something from Scooby Doo.*

"Naw," he replied. "Kids won't go near it. Animals neither."

That got my attention. Animals rely on instinct. When something signals to them, keep away, they listen. People have intellect and will ignore instinct. Then bad things happen.

I walked over to a map stand, pulled one out, and opened it on the counter as I readied my lie. "A real old west town sounds interesting. I'm a bit of a historian, and I know our order used to have a monastery near here in the 1830s. Maybe it was in Old Durango. Might be worth a visit. Could you please show me where Old Durango is?"

"Not sure why'd you want to go there, nothing to see. We got a nice little museum just down the road."

"Please," I asked again

Pops took his time but finally traced out where we were, where Durango was, and how to get to Old Durango. "County 632 is the name of the road that will get you there. Take the main road past the bridge then keep an eye out for a big pile of rocks, looks like a fat camel. That's where you turn. You should see the sign, if it ain't been shot up or torn down. If you get to an open place with lots of cacti, you've gone too far."

"So where's this old house?"

"Bout two thirds of the way to Old Durango. You can't miss it. It's maybe two hundred yards off the road on the left."

The door opened, and Brother Malachi walked in. "Have you seen Brother Vincent?"

"None of the Brethren have come in," I said. "Why?"

"Brother Gray would like your help." Code for a situation. Brother Vincent was missing.

I looked at Pops, keeping my face calm. "Pops, I think we'll just have the sodas. How much?"

After I paid, I walked out with a nonchalance I didn't feel. I kept the same pace until I made it over to where the Hammer captain was standing, preparing the others for a search.

"Captain," I said, getting the information I'd learned out in a rush, "there are two Durangos. The old one was abandoned, and has a house worth checking out. Guy running the place says it's haunted and animals won't go there." I jerked a thumb back to the shop. "You might want to have someone talk to the old guy. His name is Pops. He gave me directions to get to the old town. He's lived here forever and might know a thing or two."

"Sebastian we have a situation here."

"I understand. I'm only asking for a couple of minutes. If nothing else, we can eliminate part of our search."

I looked from his face to the others, who were staring intently at me. I didn't think they were buying my plan. I glanced at Brother Malachi, but he shook his head a little. He wasn't going to help, this was all on me. I kept going.

"We're more likely to find witches in an abandoned town than an actual city. We would've heard something by now if they were urban."

The captain frowned. I had to convince him, but not in a way that would seem like I was undermining his authority.

I leaned back a bit and partially lifted my hands, palms up. "I'm just asking for one Brother to talk to him for five minutes, see if I'm on to something. I honestly think I am, and Pops might be an asset to finding the exact location of these witches." I paused and glanced back at the shop where Pops was staring intently at our group through the window. "It'd also keep him from getting underfoot."

The captain looked at me then over to the window, nodded his head once, and said, "Good plan." He glanced at one of his men and jerked his head toward the station. The designated Hammer put down the gear and maps he'd been working with and strolled across the lot to the store.

A Hammer came up from around the back of the station and walked calmly but quickly over to the captain. "We have tracks," he said in a quiet voice, "and blood."

CHAPTER 29

The group froze and turned as one to the Hammer captain.

"Damn," he said. "Brothers Malachi, Sebastian, Stephen, and Jimmy, gear up and go with Brother Daniel here. Form two teams. Follow the trail, see what you can see. Try to avoid gunfire."

I looked up at the night sky. The moon was out, and giving off a lot of light. We'd be able to follow a good trail. The buzzer decided to go off, and I looked back over my shoulder instinctively, seeing nothing worth noting. I flushed a bit, feeling foolish, and hoping no one noticed. Luckily, they seemed more interested in gathering up their gear than in me. I grabbed my stuff and followed the group.

Maybe we can get there in time, I lied to myself.

The best we were going to do is avenge Brother Vincent. Maybe not even that. My heart beat faster and sweat formed on my head and under my arms.

At the corner of the station, near where Brother Vincent was last seen, we quickly geared up. We were out of Pop's sight and could duck around to the side of the station if anyone pulled in for gas or beer. As per our training, the other Hammers were going to stay put as a rally point. If our little team disappeared, the whole group wouldn't be lost. They'd also be able to let command know we'd run into trouble. Maybe they'd be able to help, but I doubted it.

As we did our final gear checks, one of the Hammers opened the hood of an SUV and started to poke at the engine as a diversion. The others filtered around, in the way men will, to stare at the work being done and offer unhelpful advice.

The restroom was on the back corner of the side of the building. A weak overhead light above the door gave off as much illumination as an orange cat. Skirting the light to avoid announcing our presence to whoever might be watching, Brother Daniel led us into the dark and toward a small lot of junker cars. Behind the cars were the first visible tracks and puddles that stank of blood. Using the red lens on my flashlight, we looked at the tracks, but the ground was still hard and there were no clear prints. I could tell that something had made them, but that was all. The blood glistened blackly in the red light, and the smell of it, a kind of old wet penny smell, wafted up. Brother Malachi frowned, looking worried but determined. I clicked off the light before anyone could see how worried I felt. Anything that could drag off a Hammer without making a racket was not something I wanted to meet in the dark, even with backup. Once again, we were swallowed by the gloom.

"Move out," said Brother Daniel.

The trail and blood led past the sad remnants of a fence, the wire long since gone and the posts pointing at the sky like abandoned anti-aircraft guns. The trail went into open desert. The temperature continued to drop, which made me shiver.

Brother Daniel said, "I'll stay on the trail. One team on each side. Watch the flanks." It made sense, but separated us. I really wanted to say we should stick together, but wasn't going to shame myself by offering a suggestion that might seem cowardly.

He radioed the reserve back at the gas station to let them know what we'd found and the direction we were going. Brother Malachi and I ended up on the left hand side of the trail, and we all moved out. The trail followed a straight line for about a mile then veered to the left. The moon twisted the rocks and cacti into eerie shapes. More than once, I had to double check to make sure a strange shape was inanimate.

We eased over a low hill and descended into a dark low spot. We were in some sort of small wide canyon. We followed the path, moving slowly, watching, making sure we weren't walking into an ambush. My heart was racing now, and I couldn't seem to breathe fast enough. The canyon walls were only a few feet higher than we were. Still, it was enough to block out most of the moonlight. When the buzzer went off, I almost jumped. Looking back, I saw only stars and blackness.

Brother Daniel was still in the middle, but the other team was invisible to me in the shadows. Branches of the canyon extended into the gloom, but the trail went straight down the middle, never wavering. After a few more minutes of walking, it led us to an even narrower, darker part of the canyon.

"*Hronk. Hronk. Hronk.*" The sound of an irritated monster goose echoed in front of us. It made my bladder quiver.

"Crap," said Brother Malachi softly. He got on one knee and waved me over.

I knelt beside him.

"This is going to be bad," he said, which did nothing to calm me down. He was moving his head, scanning the area while he briefed me. "We can't outrun it and we can't hide. We have to fight. Stick close to me or the others. They have better firepower than we do. It will try to separate us, and one-on-one, you'll lose. If you see it, aim for the center then move. It has a long reach. Once it goes down, use holy water, all you have."

Brother Daniel called for backup. "Five minutes," was the response. A lifetime to wait.

A giant goat-headed monstrosity erupted out of the arroyo. Sprinting for us. It was at least seven feet tall. About where the ears should've been, two horns, curled and chipped, were the watery yellow of stomach acid. Off-white fur surrounded the face, matted and speckled with blood. Purple eyes blazed in the gloom, radiating madness and death. Its chest and torso were humanish and massive. Obscenely long arms reached its knees. Goat-like legs, covered in a brown or black fur, ended in tiny hooves. In one hand, it held a stone axe that just looked wrong, as though it flowed and twisted of its own accord. It was a type of minotaur. The Greeks had made the bull-headed version famous, but there were other kinds. Minotaur may not have been a perfect translation or taxonomy, but it beat calling it a "Ram-headed beast-man." They were created by Screwfaces as a guard or set free to terrorize the local populace.

It rushed right down the trail and past us with great bounding leaps. Muzzle flashes gave the whole scene a strobe-like effect. Our silver bullets flared as they hit flesh. Several were mine, I was sure. The sounds of our bullets, trapped in our little valley, echoed and rebounded, the explosions magnified. One spent cartridge flew back and got stuck between my shirt and neck, burning the skin. The minotaur never slowed down. As it raced past Brother Daniel, it gave a seemingly lazy swing of the axe. There was a purplish flash, which made me blink and crouch. When I could see again, Brother Daniel was down. Split in two. He hadn't even had a chance to get out of the way. Blood geysered up and sank into the thirsty desert. There was a strange, sad little smile on his face.

Peace be with you, Brother.

"Up," commanded Brother Malachi.

I stood, looking all around.

"Back to back, move to the other team. We'll end up shooting each other or getting picked off."

We moved, weapons up, futilely scanning the darkness. Taking shuffling sideways steps, we moved to the other team. My heart was smashing against my chest, and I was breathing rapid short breaths, as though at a full sprint. As we got back on the trail and went past the remains of Brother Daniel, there was more gunfire. Fierce at first, it tapered off then there was a choppy scream and the night became silent again.

"Stop," said Brother Malachi in a whisper.

We waited. It would return soon enough. I was facing back the way we'd come, Brother Malachi a step away and facing the direction we were going. I thought a vehicle was coming toward us. Its lights were out, but I could just make out a boxy shape bouncing and jolting along at a good clip, the soft whine of a strained engine, and tires screeching on the sand.

"Turn..." was all the warning I got.

I pivoted as the minotaur charged. Its body was covered in blood, and one eye and most of the horn on one side had been shot away. Silver bullets embedded in magical flesh blazed but didn't seem to slow it down. It was leaping and swung its axe at me before I could do more than get off a few shots. There was a whiff of unwashed animal, and I held my MP-5 up to block the axe and dove out of the way. I rolled over and found myself holding two pieces. The edges gleamed red as though they'd been heated.

Holy crap.

I dropped the remains and drew my Glock, scanning the area. Brother Malachi had also had to scramble to get away and seemed unhurt. Worried that I'd get jumped from behind if I turned, I took a few steps backward to close the distance between us. My eyes were watering from the gasses of our bullets and the strain of trying to see in the dark. I wanted to wipe them but didn't dare move my hands from my weapon. The engine and tires let me know the SUV was much closer. I prayed it would get here before the minotaur charged again. My eyes scanned that area over and over, looking for the creature before it could strike again. There were

162

so many dark spots the minotaur could be hiding in, and the only movement was the SUV. When I shifted, I could feel the cartridge irritating and digging into my skin. The wait stretched, the strain of holding my Glock up and ready making it waver a bit. Strangely, I felt calm, ready to fight. My heart had slowed down and my breathing went back to normal.

My arms were beginning to shake when the minotaur struck again. This time it decided to attack the SUV. One moment, the rest of the team was about fifty meters away, driving fast to rescue us, and the next, the minotaur was standing on the roof, swinging its axe. The SUV braked hard, the front dipping and the back rearing up, throwing the minotaur off. It twisted in the air and landed on its feet, facing us. It charged at Brother Malachi and me again, axe held high. I fired, even though I knew that missing it could mean hitting my teammates. I could hear Brother Malachi doing the same.

With a loud roar of its engine, the SUV leaped forward and struck the minotaur hard from behind. It flew forward, sprawled out just before us, axe still in one meaty hand. I took one step to my left, and emptied my magazine into its back and head. Brother Malachi was shooting with his MP-5. Bullets dimpled flesh, the silver flaring, and blood splashed and oozed from a dozen or more wounds, but the minotaur didn't seem to notice. Even with all its damage, it was still trying to get up while I changed magazines. More Hammers rushed forward, adding their bullets. It was a long, scary moment until the creature, almost up on one knee, collapsed face-first into the desert.

"Holy water, quickly," shouted Brother Malachi.

I dropped my rucksack and pulled out my canteen of holy water. The minotaur's skin was starting to reform, to heal. The musky animal smell was much stronger, almost gagging me. My hand shook as I poured the holy water onto the creature's back. I gulped once and focused on dumping out my canteen.

More Hammers arrived, almost bumping into each other. An even stronger smell of burned lamb hit my nostrils, and my stomach heaved. Canteen empty, I stepped back past my rucksack to give myself some distance. I didn't want to shame myself by vomiting in front of everyone. I also needed to fish out that cartridge. Brother Malachi came over as I was taking deep breaths, holding up the errant cartridge as though it were important.

"Any damage?" he asked.

I shook my head, not sure I wanted to open my mouth right then. One of the Hammers approached the body with a machete. I turned away from the sight, looking out at the desert in the night, telling my ears to ignore the meaty chopping sounds of the minotaur being dismembered.

"We need to recover our Brothers," said Brother Malachi, who'd turned away as well.

"Yeah," I grunted, afraid to fully open my mouth

Breathing in the cool air settled my stomach enough to risk asking, "What do we do now? We've lost three or four of the team. Can we still function?"

"I don't know. We may have to merge with another team. We may get pulled off, but I doubt it. There are just too many witches and minions running around for Command not to use everyone."

The chopping sounds stopped. I knew from my minions class that a minotaur had to be dismembered to prevent reanimation or healing, but reading about it and seeing it up close were very different. My stomach slowly finished its flip-flopping as I breathed the night air.

"Rally up," the radio squawked, and Brother Malachi and I turned back to the SUV and walked toward it, not looking at the pile of meat.

The other SUV came up, and we began to recover our fallen. We found the remains of Brother Vincent partially eaten in the back of the arroyo. Brother Daniel and the other two members of our search party had all been bisected, which made putting the bodies into body bags a messy and disturbing process. We only said a quick prayer over the fallen, as we'd all received last rites before we left the priory. Weapons and other equipment, as well as errant brass, were retrieved, and I took Brother Daniel's MP-5 to replace my own. The Hammer captain was on the radio and cellphone at the same time, having two different conversations, reporting in what had occurred and getting instructions.

"Load up that SUV with the bodies," he said, pointing to one of the vehicles. "Brother Mike will transport them back to a collection point. He won't be rejoining us."

We moved the bodies as directed, shook hands with Brother Mike, and watched him drive off.

Part of me wanted to be the one going, but mostly I wanted payback for what had happened. I still had that calm floaty feeling, my heart rate was normal, and I was no longer sweating. We gathered around the Hammer captain.

He had a hard stern look on his face as he announced, "The mission continues. The two teams will be merged into one with me in charge and Brother Seth as my assistant. We're going to Old Durango, to the house Brother Sebastian found out about, where we'll merge with another team or two. What happens next depends on what we find there."

"What about Pops?" I asked.

"He was locking up when we got the call from Brother Daniel," said the Hammer captain. "We could barely hear the shots. Most likely, he didn't. We need to get out of here quickly in case anyone else did."

I was a bit concerned for the old guy. I don't know what the Hammers would've done if he had heard the firing. Probably nothing gentle.

We got into the SUV and drove past the now-closed gas station and back onto the road to Old Durango.

CHAPTER 30

"Master, one of my goats is dead. I believe the false monks approach," said Judith.

They were still on the porch, even though night had fallen. Thaddeus was holding court, explaining concepts to them that made their hearts race and heads reel. He nodded and continued his talk as though nothing had occurred. A short while later, his lecture was interrupted by the arrival of another supplicant.

An old, garishly-painted VW van crested a hill and entered the valley where the house stood. Conversation stopped on the porch, and as one, they turned to watch the vehicle's progress. Dust swirled, making the old car look even more decrepit. The original pink paint had faded to dull tan color, and the many stickers, with pithy slogans—*No Nukes, Respect Mother Nature, Save the Whales*—looked forlorn and pathetic. The van pulled up, brakes squealing, and with a grateful wheeze, the engine stopped. The one remaining headlight winked out, the door opened with a rusty creak, and a tall, cadaverous crone got out. She moved stiffly, as though wounded and in pain. She rubbed her hand on her worn jeans, trying to dry her sweaty palms as she limped over to the porch where the others waited. The sounds of her crunching through the hard, dry dust mingled with the wind and the creaking of wood being reformed.

She stopped short of the porch and bowed. "Master, it is good to see you again."

Thaddeus merely waited, the only sign of his agitation the creaks from the arms of the chair where he gripped them. She stood still, head bowed, shaking slightly.

The others traded glances, wondering what would happen next.

After several long minutes, Thaddeus spoke, "Gretchen, why are you here?"

"I felt the pull of your return, Master, and I was compelled to be at your side once again," she said, head still bowed.

"And why is that?"

"You are my master. Where you go, I follow."

"That hasn't always been the case. I died, and you were not there. I traveled, and you did not follow. I was tormented, and you did not join me."

"I was not here when that happened, Master," she said then added quickly, "but I've returned now."

"That's right, you weren't here. When I needed you, you were gone. Why is that?"

"I made a foolish decision," said Gretchen. The trembling increased.

Thaddeus stretched out his red arm and twirled his wrist as though stretching. Purple-black sparks danced on his fingertips. Eric and the others stepped back to make room.

"Foolish? Perhaps. Betrayal is always foolish, unless you can pull it off, which I see you can't. No. I don't think you've returned to me out of devotion, but out of desperation."

"Master, I heeded the call," she said, her voice becoming whiny.

"Very well. Let's say you did return out of a sense of loyalty. What did you bring me?"

"Just myself and information."

"What information is that, Gretchen?"

"James is on his way."

"You would speak his name in my presence?" A frown and darkening of his face was unnoticed by Gretchen, who still had her head bowed.

Thaddeus began to move, to twitch, rubbing and scratching parts of his body as though plagued by some irritant. He stood, still frowning, when a loud twang followed by a thock of wood striking wood rang out through the valley. Thaddeus and the other magi turned to see what had made the sound. A flaming ball of bones trailing greasy black smoke arced high over the valley and landed between the parked cars and the house. Instead of bouncing, the ball spun in place. The bones moved, and, with a snapping, grinding, tearing sound, began to morph into something vaguely bipedal. In response to the sounds, the house's front and side doors opened, and Judith's minions rushed out onto the porch.

Thaddeus giggled at the sight. "Prove yourself in battle, Gretchen, and all will be forgiven."

Gretchen nodded and quickly scrambled up the steps. Twangs and thocks continued to ring out, and from just over the small ridge to the south, more balls sailed into view.

Thaddeus adopted a pensive posture, arms half-crossed, eyes fixed in a thousand-yard stare. One finger tapped his forehead, deforming the skin and sinking to the second knuckle. After three hard pokes, he stopped and turned his head to Eric, who'd taken a small step back. "Eric, you did complete all the rituals properly?"

"Yes, Master, but I'm not sure they'll hold up to this."

Thaddeus pulled on one earlobe until it was stretched almost to the point of tearing free and rolled it between his fingers as though it were an errant strand of hair. "Probably not, but they will blunt the first attack."

"Master, I could send Rook to take out the launchers," said Judith.

Thaddeus released his earlobe and turned his neck until his head was almost touching his shoulder. He rolled his eyes skyward and stared for a long second. Coming to some decision, he straightened up and took a long, exaggerated step toward Judith until he was almost standing on her toes. He leaned in, forcing her to bend back. "No. There'll be a trap waiting for a counterattack, and he'll be lost. He guards the back in case this is a distraction. Have your coven spread out around the porch to watch. That takes care of three sides. Rook will stand just inside the back door. Make sure they don't leave the porch. The wards will not protect them in the yard." Thaddeus looked at Top, and screwed his face up in concentration for a second.

With a few lazy flaps of his wings, Top flew up to the roof and surveyed the area.

The minions moved out as instructed, Judith staying at Thaddeus's side with Eric and Gretchen. The first ball resolved itself into four skeletons, each holding a bone sword. They stood in place and waited. The other balls landed with crunching sounds and began to reform as well.

"Eric, you have first honors," said Thaddeus.

Eric gave a small smile. "Thank you Master," he said as he withdrew an oak stick encrusted with gems from a pocket.

The stick was snapping purple-black with magical power. Eric gripped the wand in the middle with one hand and made a punching motion toward the first skeletons. The faint outline of a gigantic fist appeared in front of the moving intruders and plowed into them. The leftmost two were hit and splintered into fragments. Eric opened his fist and, holding the wand with just his thumb, made a patting motion toward the ground. The ethereal hand, palm down, crushed the remaining skeletons into the dirt.

More balls arced through the sky and reformed into skeletons. Thaddeus nodded to Judith, who pulled a necklace out from under her leather vest. The stones were already crackling with magic. She shouted a few words of power, and a group of skeletons burst into pieces. Thaddeus turned to Gretchen and motioned for her to join the fight. Gretchen's weapon was a series of rings on her fingers that snapped and snarled with energy. She made short punching motions and skeletons were blasted across the yard in spinning pieces.

More balls were landing and turning into skeletons. Thaddeus's coven continued to attack, but the skeletons were forming faster than they could destroy them. The skeletons assembled into groups of eight and made a chattering cacophony that sounded vaguely like words.

The sounds affected the witches and warlocks. They started to slow down, to drop their guards. All except Thaddeus. He glanced right and left and a disgusted look developed on his face. From a pocket, he pulled out a rod of pure crystal, pulsing purple-black. He shouted a word of power, and swung his arm back and forth across his chest. A huge, barely visible blade formed. The point extended into the yard, the handle toward Thaddeus, as though he held it. Thaddeus moved his arms in wide motions and, with a mighty sweep, the blade crushed through skeletons, decapitating some and cutting through the chest of others. They crumpled in piles and were silenced. The other magi, recovering from the spell, shook their heads and renewed their attacks. Soon there was nothing left but piles of bones, which were quickly disintegrating.

Thaddeus rolled his eyes up, as though receiving a message, and said, "We have skinned wolves on the way. Bertrand has come to play."

Eric had a worried look on his face. "Master, are we ready to handle him?"

Thaddeus whirled toward the necromancer. "You need to stop doubting my powers." His eyes blazed and his face started to elongate and become thinner. His chin formed into a beak-like point and his nose shrank until it was just two slits. Eric and the others took an involuntary step back. Thaddeus's skin was a maelstrom as the tattoos swirled and reformed into even more hideous and maddening shapes. Gretchen stared a bit too long and fell to the floor of the porch, thrashing and flopping, a stream of urine dripping on the wood. None of the other magi even looked in her direction.

Thaddeus's eyes grew bulbous and black, and when he opened his mouth to speak, he revealed serrated teeth. "There are more things hidden in the dark places than you could ever imagine. I have become one of them."

The magi still standing fell to their knees in obeisance and awe. Thaddeus, ignoring their supplications, reached down and grabbed Gretchen by the hair and dragged her out into the yard. Each step left burned imprints in the ground, and smoke rose in his wake.

"You were always weak," he said to the convulsing witch, "but at least you will have some use now." With one hand, he held her upright.

Gretchen continued to twitch and jerk spasmodically. Drool dripped down her face and her eyes had rolled back into her head. He spoke words of power, raised a clenched fist, blazing purple-black, and opened it. The flames grew even higher. Thaddeus placed his hand on her chest then slipped it through her breastbone and into her body. With a twist, he ripped out Gretchen's heart. She let out a keening wail and sank in a boneless heap at Thaddeus's feet when he dropped her. He raised the heart over his head, chanting.

"*Natrllgah voqr gherrk*," he said over and over, getting louder until his voice rose into a shriek.

Thaddeus squeezed the heart with both hands. Flaming blood dripped onto his upturned face. The flames were absorbed into his skin, and Thaddeus began to grow. He didn't become much taller, but thicker, heavier, more substantial. When he finished the ritual, he threw the mangled muscle at the corpse.

Gretchen's body blazed with fire and was quickly consumed, leaving a small charred spot and some ash on the ground.

Thaddeus turned back toward the house. "Get up fools," he said to the magi still on their knees. "I'll take point. You make sure nothing gets past me. Hit me with any of your puny power, and I'll end you."

He turned away from the shaken magi and waited. The skinned wolves trotted down to the valley floor and formed a line. They were large, powerful beasts, each the size of a small horse. A figure strode up behind them, silhouetted in the moonlight.

"Bertrand," shouted Thaddeus. "Surrender or die."

The magus didn't respond. Bertrand looked around for a second and made a shooing motion with both arms. The skinned wolves began their charge.

CHAPTER 31

James

My car shimmied and skidded along the dirt and potholes as I slowly got closer to the house. Looking back in the rearview mirror, I saw Glaive sitting there, unaffected by the rocking and bouncing. The shortest route to Old Durango was a modern, paved two-lane road coming in from the north-east, but I wasn't about to use that one. I was headed in from the south and had already run into many other magi, so the main road was sure to be chock-full of them. There was also the possibility that my former Brethren were on the trail as well. I was attempting to approach the house from the south using an old tertiary road I'd learned about after fleeing my mutiny. The road was on the other side of a ridgeline from the house. A long time ago, some tectonic upheaval had created a line of hills. This part of the road was cut close to the ridge, even though there was no drop off and plenty of flat space. Forced to drive slowly to avoid wrecking, I ended up sneaking into the camp without being noticed.

I came around a sharp bend in the road, expecting to go another half-mile or so before I had to walk the rest of the way, when I almost collided with an ogre standing next to a catapult. There were four catapults in a line, each manned by an ogre. A bit behind them, and on the other side of the road, was a large cauldron, belching steam. The fire underneath was down to the last few sticks—black hickory, pre-burned, and then covered in ritual tar. I knew well the requirements for heating a cauldron. Bones, stacked next to the cauldron, had dirt and scraps of clothes attached to them, as though they'd been recently disinterred. A witch was walking away from the cauldron toward a pavilion-style canvas tent, holding a large tome in her hands. I saw this all in a flash as I braked hard.

"Glaive," I said. "Kill everything."

He was out of the car before it even completely stopped, swords in his hands. The ogre turned and the surprised look on his face was greeted by the first sword. Glaive wove an intricate pattern, and the ogre was reduced to chunks. Glaive was already moving to the next creature as the pieces hit the ground. Using the car for cover, I checked to make sure nothing was behind me, faced front, and fired. The witch had looked up to see what was going on and caught the first burst. Bullets stitched into her side and head, twirling her a bit. I shot her again, and she wavered for a moment before sinking to her knees and collapsing face-first into the dirt. I shifted to target the farthest ogre as I didn't want to hit Glaive or let him get ganged up on. The three remaining ogres would probably tear him apart if they could attack at once. They'd seen what Glaive had done and rushed toward him. Glaive ran lightly at the second ogre, taking large hops, almost like a little girl skipping to the candy store.

The second ogre was also messily reduced to long slabs of meat and gristle by Glaive's swords, but the third was approaching him fast. He only got a few steps when my first rounds hit him. I was aiming for the face to put him down fast, and my practice paid off. He suddenly stopped running, braking so hard and fast he almost fell over. A round must've gone into his open mouth, because it slammed shut and he clapped his hands over it. There was a bewildered expression on his face as blood leaked from between his hands. I let loose another burst. The ogre turned to one side and fell over in a heap. The remaining ogre had body-checked Glaive, who was knocked off his feet by the collision, but not before getting in a few slashes. I shifted aim before the ogre could follow up and opened fire again. I wasn't as lucky this time. My rounds hit his chest, painful but not lethal, and the ogre looked up at me for just a second. Glaive swiped one sword at the ogre's legs. Bone broke with a crack, and Glaive rolled away from the ogre and onto his feet. I couldn't get a clear shot so I scanned for other targets, while Glaive finished it off.

There was no other movement, and the tent door remained clear. I did another quick check behind me then watched Glaive as he made sure the witch and ogres I'd shot stayed dead by chopping the bodies into steak-sized pieces. The meaty twacks sounded like a butcher hard at work. Once that was done, Glaive approached the tent, swords up. I should've known it far too easy.

Glaive weaved around a half-buried boulder, and that was when the metal sprite attacked. It wasn't fully grown, only five feet or so, but it was big enough. Two squat legs propelled it forward. Made of a shiny, silvery metal, the body was large and round, with long arms almost dragging on the ground. It had no head; its eyes and huge mouth were in its body. Glaive reacted at once, swinging both swords at the sprite. One sword bounced off the body while the other went into the mouth and was bitten off. The sprite latched onto Glaive with its hands and began to liquefy his limbs. Glaive struggled but was held fast. Drops of molten metal snapped and hissed as they contacted the ground.

"*Master,*" shrieked Glaive as the sprite tore him in two.

I'd dropped my weapon and brought up the severed hand, but by then it was too late. I spoke the words of power needed and a bolt of electricity tore into the sprite, blowing it into pieces. I fired another bolt at what was left of Glaive, to make sure Steel wasn't able to extract revenge before returning to the earth. The shriek rang inside my head as Steel was obliterated as well. Stray current arced back and forth between the parts until grounding out.

A brief moment of irritation washed over me, as I would have to go back to my original plan. The loss of Glaive was a nuisance, but if he couldn't even handle a half-grown metal sprite, perhaps it was for the best that I didn't have him holding me back.

I checked the camp and found nothing else worth noting. It was time to see what Thaddeus was up to and finish him off. If I could.

CHAPTER 32

Sebastian

The wheels hummed, and the SUV bounced along toward whatever was next. The vehicle smelled of sweat, cordite, and nervousness. Or maybe it was just me. Brother Malachi was silent, his eyes closed, though I wasn't sure if he was thinking or trying to rest. My calm had been replaced by anxiety. I wanted to talk, to discuss what had happened, or the latest baseball scores, anything to avoid dwelling on the minotaur and the deaths in our team—the sick stomach-churning feeling that I was out of my league. A dozen times, I started to speak or reach out to him, but stopped short. Even though I felt weak, I wasn't going to show it. I tried closing my eyes, but they just sprang back open. Looking out the side windows did nothing as the landscape was devoid of anything worth observing. Just the occasional road that seemed to lead nowhere and the desert—empty expanses made sinister by the moonlight.

Dammit, get yourself together. You've already failed once in this life. Do you want everyone to know you're ready to run like a scared girl?

That thought brought me out of my funk. There was no way I could let the others know how I felt. Turning in the back seat until I could look behind us, I stared out the window, watching the dust swirl along. To keep myself from getting morbid, I thought about my days as a novice with Rubin, Maurice, and Thomas.

The memories brought a smile to my face. Rubin was now in Philadelphia, Maurice was a roamer in the Eastern part of Pennsylvania, and Thomas stayed at the monastery as an intel member.

And what about you? What have you done? I thought bitterly.

No, I replied to myself, sick of the self-doubt and poor-me attitude. It wasn't like me. I was better than this. Hadn't I shown it time and time again? I had the ring. Others believed in me. Maybe it was time I believed in myself. I looked down at my ring and spun it around my finger, watching the gold and black flash.

I will not fail again. I will never give anyone a reason to doubt me again. If I die, it won't be because I hesitated.

Thus resolved, I felt better, stronger, and sat up straighter in my seat.

We joined up with another convoy of vehicles just short of our turn off to Old Durango. They fell in behind us as we bounced along.

"We have point until we get to the jump off position," said the Hammer captain, moving the headset away from his mouth for a moment. A few nudges and everyone was focused on him. He'd spent the drive time getting reports and passing along the information to Brother Seth, letting everyone else sleep, if they could. "Team B behind us is led by the Master Hammer. There's another group waiting just up the road. Everyone is headed to the house Sebastian clued us in on. We have more confirmation that it's the location of this convergence. Supposedly, it's Thaddeus."

My stomach flopped, and I began to sweat. Thaddeus. The man who'd tortured me. Who'd gotten into my brain and pried out my memories. Every embarrassing moment or thought I'd ever had was exposed and mocked. When that was done, he'd told me what I'd really done in that back room in Providence. I hadn't ended the suffering of a tortured woman by killing her, an action I'd thought had stained my soul forever. It was worse. I had forgiven and asked for God's intercession for the witch who'd destroyed my family. The witch who'd killed my wife and unborn child, set fire to our house, and framed me for it. I forgave her and asked God to do the same. Then I ended her torment, thinking I'd committed a cardinal sin. There is no forgiveness for cardinal sins in this life, and I was sure I was headed for Hell when I died. When Thaddeus told me what'd I done, that instead of avenging my wife, as I'd vowed to do, I'd blessed the witch, I'd wanted to die. Hoped I would. As if that weren't enough, he'd robbed me of the ability to understand music,

175

destroying the memories I held most dear: my wife playing her cello. I was rescued before I turned, but I was broken. He'd beaten me. I lay there in my kennel, naked and shivering, not caring what happened next. I'm still not sure if I've healed from that time. Or if I ever will. My face flushed, not in shame, but with hatred.

"Thaddeus," said Brother Malachi, giving me a shake. "Are you ready to face this?"

Anger swept aside fear and self-loathing. I turned to my mentor. "Oh, yes," I said, practically spitting out the words through clenched teeth. "I want to Put him to the Question and Purge him. His time here needs to end."

Brother Malachi peered deeply into my eyes. My answer was awkward, formulaic, and must've worried him. I stared back, sweat running down my forehead until my eyes stung and I had to blink.

"We have to do this as a team."

"I know. It'll be enough to Purge him."

"I'm serious. If you try anything by yourself, you could screw up the whole mission. He's too powerful. Hell, even with all we have, he might still get away."

I just nodded, ignoring him. I'd get Thaddeus. *Even if it costs me my life,* I vowed silently.

"This won't bring her back, or change what he did," he said softly.

"I know," I said, my throat tightening, "but if I don't try, I'll never be whole. I'll never be able to forget." What I said next was a lie, but had to be said to avoid being sidelined. The words tasted bitter. "But maybe I can heal. Maybe forgive myself for losing her, again." I looked down, not wanting him to see the tears.

He patted me on the shoulder. "We'll do what we can. God willing, we'll hunt him down and end him forever."

When I looked back up, a group of SUVs was waiting for us. "That's team C," called out the Hammer captain as we went past them and kept going. He was again alternating between the radio and phone, coordinating with the other teams and the Priory.

"Three minutes out," said the team leader. "We're going to be Assault with Team B. Team C will be flanking. They'll be using machine guns as a base of support and a couple of snipers. Make sure you stay together in line. Get too far ahead, and you'll be seeing the baby Jesus."

The expression was so absurd, I almost laughed. *Who the hell says the baby Jesus these days?*

The team leader didn't have a twang or the slow cadence of the Deep South, and I wondered where he'd picked up the expression. I stopped my musing as, rapid fire, he rattled off names and positions, frequencies, alternative sites, rally points, and recovery locations. Brothers triple-checked their equipment. I was one of them.

CHAPTER 33

James

With the loss of Glaive, I had to go back to my original plan. Combat between witches is usually face to face, and there was no way I'd risk that kind of battle. I needed distance, and to use all the skills I'd learned, both as a magi and one of the Brothers. I went to my trunk and pulled the rifle out of its case. The spring-loaded bipod snapped into position. With a small snort, I stopped trying to grab the case of ammo and deliberately refolded the legs, making sure the retaining clip held the bipod against the stock of the rifle.

This is why I need an assistant. Maybe I should've brought Olivia along. It would've been easy to enthrall her. I closed my eyes to stop this train of thought. *Olivia was a means to an end. Nothing more. Stay on task. Only the weak worry about what-ifs.*

After grabbing the box of ammo, I left the car behind. The hillside wasn't steep but seemed to go on for a very long time. About halfway up, I saw the stairs traveling from the valley floor to the top of the hill and sidled over to them. Someone had forced the land to reform into a series of flat surfaces, each a little higher than the previous one. Checking for traps only took a second and showed me the way was clear. A strong magus had either bidden something to make these steps, or reshaped the land personally.

It'd take a lot of power to do that, I thought, grinning. *Looks like Thaddeus has some problems other than me.*

Deciding there was no reason to do otherwise, I took the steps. Just before I reached the top, I saw the stylized 'B' carved into a rocky portion.

Figures, I thought as I climbed, *only Bertrand would be arrogant enough to actually sign his work.*

I knew of Bertrand from stories told by other magi, sly words from the summoned, the odd reference or two from oracles. Thaddeus hated him for existing. Most witches keep quiet about their age, what they studied, their origins, lest it be turned against them. Bertrand was so powerful, he ignored all of that. He let everyone know his story and actually used the information to keep rivals at bay. It was a warning; he'd been around a very long time, and slain many who'd challenged him.

Bertrand had come to power during the French Revolution, when the Committee of Public Safety was foolishly killing priests by the dozens. The few magi in hiding to avoid being Purged were suddenly able to move about, collect followers, influence and increase the savagery of France tearing itself apart in the name of Reason. Bertrand claimed he'd sensed an end to the madness and left, but more likely he'd had to flee. In any event, he ended up in New Orleans. There, he eliminated or outlasted all his competitors, until he was Ruler of the Magi for all of South Louisiana. Every hedge witch, voodoo practitioner, po' doctor, and warlock paid him rent and servitude, or died.

Bertrand took in the occasional acolyte, trained them, and then sent them out into the world. His ego was such that they were all renamed Bertrand, even the witches. They left his mentoring powerful and dangerous, and it further spread his story. Our trip to New Mexico had been to get enough power for Thaddeus to master Bertrand. And not just beat him, but defeat him in New Orleans, at the seat of his power.

With Bertrand here, facing off against Thaddeus, the odds of my survival had just gone way up.

The stairs ended in a flat surface at the top of the hill. I had an excellent view of the valley where the house lay, not to mention the battle going on. I quickly dropped into a prone position and scanned the area. The moon was out and gave me enough light to see shapes. The house was still there, but seemed less decrepit—the sagging was gone and the lines were straight and true. On the porch, several people were fighting off some creatures and losing. It took a second's concentration to realize they were skinned wolves. A serious beast not easily summoned or controlled. Bertrand was a real player indeed.

I swung the rifle around, looking through the scope, scanning. Someone, or something, stood in the front yard, alone. Another figure was striding away from me. Focusing on the one standing in the yard, I knew right away who it was. Thaddeus. He was different: bigger and more substantial somehow. His face and body were transformed into something new, feral and dangerous, but I knew it was him. A quick shift, and I saw the walking figure, another mage, probably Bertrand, still moving toward Thaddeus, seemingly unconcerned. Shifting back to Thaddeus, I watched him finishing off some of the skinned wolves. It hurt to look at him, and my eyes watered. I moved my head and blinked rapidly. Thaddeus wasn't weak, bereft of power. If anything, he was even stronger than before. Probably stronger than Bertrand.

I didn't have much time. Thaddeus would kill Bertrand, and then it would be my turn. I prepped as fast as I could, knowing I'd get one shot. Back in my days as a sniper for the Brethren, I would take time to get everything perfect, making minute adjustments and waiting for a shot. I didn't have that luxury now. The shot wasn't far, maybe five hundred meters, but the real problem was time, and if Thaddeus could even be killed. His new shape worried me. Keeping my eyes on Thaddeus—indirectly, to avoid the stinging sensation I got when I stared at him—I loaded a round into the chamber by touch. It was a special round, copper-sided with a silver tip and core, and death powder inside. The death powder was made by sacrificing an infant and grinding up the skull then infusing the shards with malicious spirits. Mine were some bums I'd tormented until they died. Mad beyond measure, they'd hollow out Thaddeus and strip him of his magic.

I eased the bolt forward and made my final adjustments, waiting for the shot to line up. The sky flashed with the purple-black of magic. Thaddeus merely stood there, the faint glimmer of a shield in front of him. I let out a breath and, during that pause, squeezed the trigger. The rifle roared, but hardly moved. Through the scope, I saw Thaddeus flung back, seemingly in two pieces. On instinct, I worked the bolt and loaded another round, while I shifted the view, looking for my next shot: Bertrand.

He was running toward the pieces of Thaddeus. Just as I had him in my sights and was ready to fire, he ducked down into a small gully and was lost from view.

The sounds of angry, straining engines rumbled through the valley. I looked up to see the headlights of several vehicles charging the house. My former Brothers come to Purge witches.

Time to go.

I was safe, and Thaddeus would stay dead this time. Before, he'd had his magic, even if he was in pieces. The death powder would steal his magic, the mad bums' spirits would eat his flesh, and he'd have nothing, be nothing, when he got to Hell.

Now I just had to decide if I wanted to slink back to Taos and my banal life there with Olivia, or return to the life I was meant for: ruling the mundane sheeple. It wasn't a hard decision. Who says no to being a god?

As I stood, a net engulfed me. Silver barbs dug into my flesh. My magic was snuffed out. I tried to struggle, but the silver burned, blistering my exposed skin, and sapping me of my strength. My skin was on fire, my head overloaded with screaming torment, and muscles useless. It was like I'd been hit with a Taser.

No fair, I thought. *Thaddeus didn't react this way to the manacles.*

My torso folded over then my knees gave out. I hit the ground hard, dealing with the pain and trying to swallow my fear. I tried to reach for my pistol, but couldn't move. It hurt to blink, to think. I was trapped. A figure walked up to me.

"Hello, husband," said my wife.

CHAPTER 34

James

What the hell is she doing here?

I thought I'd been nabbed by another magus or even the Poor Brothers, but my wife?

"Olivia," I stammered, having to concentrate to speak.

She came closer, dressed in blue jeans and a black shirt, and with her gloved hands gripping a pistol. Her eyes gleamed in a way I'd never seen before. A doll on a leash rode on her shoulder. Black, beady eyes stared at me, and it smiled with jagged cloth teeth. A Hoganna doll, one possessed by a spirit. Sometimes wise, sometimes a potent weapon, but always leading the owner to madness. My eyes bounced between Olivia and the doll as I tried to understand. I'd never seen this doll before, never smelled any magic in the house or seen its purple-black aura. It was impossible. How could I not have seen it?

"How-How did you get a Hoganna doll?"

Olivia gave me a little smile, and leaned her head toward the doll. "It was a gift. Something I got just before I met you."

"A gift? From who?"

"Thaddeus, of course."

The doll gave off a shrill little-girl cackle. "Stab him, cut out his eyes. He never loved you. He used you."

Olivia stroked its hair absently as she seemed to consider the suggestion.

I tried again to move, to retrieve the severed hand in my jacket pocket, but the silver was so heavy and draining.

"Not true," I said, trying not to whine. "I did love you. I made you feel alive. You said so. I helped you. I helped with your son, and I never betrayed you."

"My son is a fat, slovenly, ignorant lump. He's a burden and a drain. I'll probably sacrifice him when I'm done here."

The doll laughed again. "Yes. Yes, kill the boy and be free," it shrilled.

Olivia continued, not even really looking at me. "Maribell has told me many things. She's my oracle. She told me about you before we even met. She said you would never love me, but I should take you in anyway. So I did. And what she said was true. Did you ever help me, did you use your powers for me? No. Maribell did. She helped me solve crimes. She helped me get rid of Sergeant Chanber. Not you. You were too busy hiding. With her, I'll become police chief, or maybe mayor."

"I would've helped. But I thought you were happy."

She turned to look at me, her chest heaving and her eyes now gleaming red. "I wanted more you bastard. I deserved more. I took you in. I made sure you were safe. And you did nothing. Just occupied my bed and ate my food. Another thief. Stealing my life, stabbing me in the back every time you didn't help me. Killing me each second you were around." She blinked a few times and looked back at the doll.

It patted her head with its stumpy cloth arm in a comforting sort of way.

Calm again, she looked back at me. "She told me all about you. Maribell introduced me to Thaddeus while he was trapped. He told me about your betrayal and how it was only a matter of time before you killed me as well."

"You...you talked to him?"

"Yes. Thaddeus promised me many things if I would just do one small favor for him. But I had to wait until he returned."

"You're too late. I've killed him."

"Perhaps," she said, "but I will uphold my end of the bargain. Even if he's in Hell, you'll soon be joining him."

"Olivia," I pleaded, trying to stall, to buy time.

"Till death do us part," she said with a serene smile on her face.

She aimed the pistol at my head and pulled the trigger.

No. No, not like this, it's not supposed to happen this way. Not to me.

Brilliant white light flared in my mind's eye, followed by purple-black flames. Laughter welcomed me to Hell.

CHAPTER 35

Sebastian

The vehicles came around a corner and entered a flat area occupied by a house and several beat-up cars. The first group of SUVs turned off the road onto the valley floor, bumping over the small gullies that crisscrossed it. They fanned out, raising huge plumes of dust. We turned off the road as well, forming a rank. Once all the SUVs were abreast, we accelerated, aimed at the house. I looked past my Brethren, through the windshield, at our destination. In the bright moonlight, I could see we were headed to an old style two-story house with a wide wraparound porch. It seemed wrong even from the SUV. Its angles and planes were off, with parts bulging out and corners that didn't seem to meet up properly. It was as though I were looking at it through a warped lens. Blots of purple-black erupted in the sky, obscuring the moonlight.

This is it, I thought, just before the SUV flipped over. One moment we were racing toward the house and then there was a second of weightlessness as we inverted. We flipped back over front. Gear that was resting on the floor rained down on us. The SUV crunched down onto the roof, and we slide for a bit rear-first before we came to a stop. Quite a few un-monk-like curses were uttered as we tried to crawl out the doors. I had to kick the back doors several times, fragmenting the glass, to force them open wide enough to escape. Gunfire cracked out, the battle was on, and I was stuck.

Move. Move. Hurry, or you'll die.

My foot hurt, but I didn't care. I didn't want to go out this way, not trapped in a big metal coffin. I kicked the door again and again, slowly shoving it open. Finally, there was enough room, and I moved. Crawling through the half-opened doors, I kept down until I got to a corner of the next SUV in line. I took a knee, staying low, only half-aiming my MP-5. A glance back showed me Brother Malachi coming out behind me.

"Motherfucking, son of a bitch, damned to Hell piece of shit," he growled as he wriggled free.

My mouth hung open.

"Get firing, you moron. Do you want to die?" he said when he saw me.

I snapped my head forward and looked for a target to engage. My hands were sweaty, and I was breathing fast.

In the far distance, I saw a glowing man and opened fire. I thought I hit him, but without effect. The man reached into a pocket; pulled something out, and hurled it in my direction while ducking down into a gully. The object bounced twice and exploded. A shaft of green light erupted from the ground in a V shape, opening a rift in the night air. Screaming, as loud as a freight train, sounded, and a sickly-yellow monster charged out of the rift.

The ground caught fire when it stepped out. One giant eye in the middle of its forehead glowed purple-black as it looked around. At least eight feet tall, it had three legs, bat-like wings on its back, and it swung a scythe in one malformed hand. Opening its impossibly large tentacle-rimmed mouth, it let off another scream. It was headed right for me.

I opened fire on it, keeping tight shot groups, aiming for the head. Flares erupted as the silver caught fire, but it kept shambling to where I crouched and fired. It took a dozen long steps at a sprint, when a machine-gun burst caught it on one side. The creature stumbled, taking a few sideways steps and turning as it regained its balance. The machine gun opened up on it again, knocking it back, causing it to waver. The creature rebalanced, and turned toward what was hurting it. It screamed one more time and raised the scythe over its head in apparent defiance. It charged the machine gun, forgetting me. I kept firing at it, tracking it as it moved.

"Sebastian, back to the portal," yelled Brother Malachi.

I swung back as another creature came out. It was an even larger version of the first.

"Mag," I yelled as I'd run dry.

I was changing out for a fresh one when I heard, "Grenade," and dropped flat. Too scared of looking up and seeing a monster standing over me, I didn't follow my training and duck my head. I watched the grenade's path as it arced out, low over the ground. Well thrown, the grenade bounced once, ending up knee high and right next to the leg of the second creature, when it exploded.

The flash blinded me for a second, and the crack sounded muted. Blinking furiously to get rid of the afterimage, I pointed my weapon in the direction of the portal. The creature had a leg blown off and was trying to get up. I rose onto one knee and rammed the fresh magazine home. The heavier boom of sniper rifles echoed, machine guns chattered, and more grenades exploded. I kept blinking smoke and sweat out of my eyes.

Die. Die. Die.

I squeezed the trigger again and again, firing until I was out. Next to me, Brother Malachi fired in short, choppy bursts. Bullets from other directions struck the creature over and over. Flares from the silver spread like wildfire all over its body. Burning flesh melted off it and dripped onto the ground. Dark fluid painted the area around it, yet it still struggled to stand. Finally a round hit it right in its giant eye, exploding it like a popped zit. The creature flopped back and lay flat, only twitching from the impact of bullets.

The portal flared and winked out of existence. As I was changing magazines again, the body caught fire, shimmering in the flames, before fading into nothingness.

"Form up," said a small, tinny voice, and I realized my earpiece had fallen out at some point. I crammed it back into my ear to listen to what was going on as Brother Malachi spoke, diverting my attention.

"Sebastian, help me up," he said as I stood. I extended an arm, and he grabbed my hand and pulled himself up, facing me, leaving his weapon on the ground. "My left arm's dislocated. I need you to put it back in place." His shoulder was hunched and deformed.

The sight made my stomach gurgle in discomfort. "Brother—" I didn't know what to say. He needed my help, but once again, I was unsure of myself.

"Just do it, and I'm sorry for snapping at you."

We'd had extensive training in first aid and care in addition to our anatomy classes, but I'd never done this before.

You can do this. Be fast.

I glanced around quickly to make sure nothing was sneaking up on us before I set my weapon down. Placing both hands at the top of his left arm, I felt for the hyper-extension. Sweat was pouring down Brother Malachi's pale face.

How the hell could he fire with an arm out of the socket? I thought. *I'd probably just lie there and cry.*

"Ready?" I asked, and he nodded. A quick tug, and it slid right back into place.

"Fucking monkey shit," swore Brother Malachi as the arm gave a loud pop. He gave me a sidelong glance and apologized for swearing. I barely noticed, surprised by how easy it had been.

"It was the shoulder talking." He rotated his arm while I picked up my MP-5.

He did the same, but slower, as the command, "Move out in line," came over the radio. We glanced around and sidled into the line moving out toward the house. Still looking back every few steps, I could see figures around the SUVs, helping injured Brethren and, in some cases, dragging away bodies. Ours was the only SUV that had flipped over, but other SUVs had crushed bumpers and looked as though they'd plowed into a wall.

Explosions from the back of the house *crumped* out in the night.

"Does anyone have eyes on the back?" asked Brother Malachi.

"Negative," was the reply.

Brother Malachi and I stopped at the sound of explosions. We were no longer part of the line but had fallen a few steps back. It saved us.

CHAPTER 36

Thaddeus laughed as the skinned wolves charged down the hill, picking up speed. Their bodies were the size of ponies with a vague lupine look about them, and they had faces that were more of an alligator's elongated snout, but with tusk-like canines that stuck out from their lips. Long legged, but with knees that bent backward, they took short hops and leaps over gullies, moving faster and faster. The hairless rat-like tails were streaming behind them like a rope pennant as they rushed forward. Their skin was thin and translucent, displaying what they'd last eaten and the beating of their hearts.

Two angled toward Thaddeus and the rest veered toward the house. He wasn't concerned about what happened to the rest of his coven. If they died, they were weak and he'd get other servants. There were always more ready to serve. Thaddeus waited until the two skinned wolves were closer then pulled out his wand. With a sinuous motion, a wave of purple-black raced to the creature, knocking it down. It wrapped around the skinned wolf like a constrictor and kept squeezing until the wolf split in half.

The second kept going, driven forward by Bertrand's command. When it was in range, it leaped. Thaddeus caught it by the throat, snatching it out of the air. The skinned wolf's legs kicked as Thaddeus choked it, all the while staring at Bertrand's approaching figure.

"Weak," taunted Thaddeus.

The skinned wolf's jaw opened and its tongue jutted out. With a crunch, Thaddeus broke its neck. He opened his hand, letting the creature fall to his feet, and began to speak again when he was hit by the bullet.

The force of it threw him out of his new body, and he landed in two pieces. The new body tried to rise, to shake off the damage, but the death powder and silver were too much. The body blanched white, starting where the bullet had struck and spreading rapidly. Seeing in an instant that the new body was doomed, Thaddeus retrieved the rest of his mind from his puppet and let the body shrivel. He was starting to get up when the SUVs arrived. Bertrand had ducked down in one of the little gullies that crisscrossed the yard and wasn't visible. He glanced quickly back up at the porch. The wolves were down, but several of his servants were no longer standing. Thaddeus quietly spoke a few words of power and walked back toward the house, his shield preventing anyone from seeing him. He'd let Bertrand deal with the false monks while he waited and either finished off the rest or made good his escape. He'd lost a lot of power when his new body died and needed time to replenish.

He'd taken three steps when one of his minions told him what had happened to James. He gave a small smile as he kept walking.

Foolish boy. Too stupid to understand plans within plans. I was more than ready when you led that pathetic rebellion. I almost cried with happiness when it occurred.

He enjoyed the sensation of victory for two more steps before he finished the plan. Olivia had been a nice puppet, but it was time for her to go.

"*Detonate,*" he commanded, and a brief flash of purple-black flared over the ridge off to the south.

The clap of the explosion came a fraction of a second later. Thaddeus walked through the wards, feeling them hum with power for a brief instant as he breached them. He had to step around the remains of a skinned wolf and a couple of Judith's nameless minions. A few more steps, and he was on the porch. Only Eric and Judith were still there waiting for him, looking at the yard but unable to see him.

Thaddeus said, "Get inside," and marched past them, turning off his shield.

Judith informed Thaddeus of the losses. Rook had failed in the end and was brought down by three skinned wolves. There were just two members of Judith's coven left, both useful only for sacrifice. Top had not been seen since going up to the roof as a lookout.

Thaddeus thought for a moment. "Top's still watching. Bertrand's also still out there. Hidden, for the moment. The false monks have arrived."

Eric went white, and Judith looked down at the floor.

"The monks should be stopped by the outer ward, but the inner ward is only for magi Master," said Eric haltingly.

"Yes, I know, fool," snapped Thaddeus. "They'll come in a line, and the outer ward will take care of many. Bertrand will finish off the rest." The pause was interrupted by a purple-black flash and the sounds of crashes. And then a silence.

"Go to a window and tell me what's happening," said Thaddeus, waving an arm at Judith. "Eric, you cover the back."

The two moved off and peered out windows. Gunfire erupted out of the stillness.

"Master, the monks have deployed and are shooting at Bertrand," said Judith. "He's thrown something and is running." Another flash, this time a sickly green, flared through the windows. "He's opened a portal," said the witch. "He's summoned a gut ripper." The sounds of gunfire increased.

Thaddeus, who'd been pacing, stopped and looked up, a line creasing his forehead. He suddenly felt cold. "What?" he said. "Let me see." He rushed to the window.

"There's a second one," said Judith, pointing.

Thaddeus slapped her away.

Judith flew from the window and hit the wall, leaving a dent before sinking to the floor, stunned.

Thaddeus went back to staring out the window. His eyes grew wide at the sight, and sweat dotted his upper lip. Fear knotted his guts—a sensation he'd not felt in many years. More guns fired, getting louder and closer.

"Not possible," he said in a whisper as Judith slowly picked herself up. "How could he be that strong?"

The first gut ripper managed to reach a knot of the monks and swung twice. Chunky fluids sailed through the air as the two monks were flung backward by the force of the disemboweling. The gut ripper paused for a second, turned, and started to collapse. A white flash made Thaddeus turn back to the portal. The second gut ripper was down as well, and the portal wavered.

The portal closing was a stroke of luck for him—the longer it was open, the more gut rippers would emerge. A wave of relief washed over Thaddeus. He wasn't sure he would've been able to battle a horde of gut rippers. Monks formed up in a line and advanced.

191

He glanced at Judith, who was crouched nearby, alternating between looking out the window and looking at Thaddeus.

"See. Just as I predicted. So locked in their battle plans, and so easy to—"

"Master," screamed Eric.

Several explosions came from the back of the house, and as Thaddeus turned, a wave of sickly green rushed toward him.

CHAPTER 37

Sebastian

The first two Hammers to hit the wall were flung back a dozen feet. One moment they were walking forward, the next they were limp, flying through the air, ripples of electricity stretching between them and a ward. Finally, their bodies were too far for the bolts to follow, and the lightning snapped back to a putrid orange, semi-solid wall of tainted air. Ripples of electricity, like lightning bolts underwater, crackled where the two Hammers had made contact, following an arc that described a circle around the house. The bolts sizzled away, fading from sight. A few seconds later, so did the wall. There was a pause as everyone stared at what had just happened.

"Stop," yelled Brother Malachi over the radio. "There's a power wall. Use your holy water, if you have any left." The two Brethren had hit hard. They didn't get back up, and the smell of cooked flesh wafted out into the night.

"Medic," I called over the radio.

Probably useless.

It wasn't like everyone hadn't seen the strike, but it was habit from my training to call for a medic when someone went down.

The line stopped, and Hammers pulled canteens out. Those who were out of holy water, like myself, took a knee and kept our weapons up and ready in case a target presented itself. More sounds came from the house, crashing and crunching, as though an enraged rhino was doing its best to demolish its prison. Flashes of purple-black were visible through the windows. Screaming rent the night, along with the sounds of breaking glass.

"Looks like a fight's going on in there," I said to Brother Malachi.

"Good. Makes our job easier," he replied.

The canteens, tops open, trailing water, were flung toward the house. They sailed through the air, encountering nothing. One particularly well-thrown one landed on the porch. The holy water spilled out, and where it made contact with the wood, flames erupted. More flashes of magic lit up the inside of the house, some boring holes through the walls and roof.

"Hold tight," commanded Brother Malachi. He wasn't in charge, but it was a smart order. If the witches had a falling out and decided to kill each other, we'd be able to finish off the remainder.

Good idea.

I wasn't about to say it, that would be too close to admitting my fear, but I was very ready to stay right where I was for the moment. There was no point risking lives if we didn't have to. More Hammers had taken a knee, like myself; some were even lying on the ground. All had their weapons up and ready. I stayed on one knee, mimicking Brother Malachi. After a few seconds, I switched knees; my brand was rubbing.

More flashes, even larger and more vivid, burst from the house. Purple-black shapes bored through the house and into the night. Entire chunks of wall and roof were blown away. The flames were quickly consuming the front porch.

A figure on fire ran through one of the holes in the side of the house. She was screaming, an animalistic keening that rose higher and louder. I'd never heard anything like it before. It didn't sound like anything a human could make, and the hair on the back of my neck stood up. Molten pieces of her dripped off as she tried to escape. With every step, she left behind a flaming puddle of herself. She kept running, fanning the flames higher. When the machine guns opened up, it was a mercy.

"Eyes front," commanded Brother Malachi, and I tore myself away from the awful sight lying in a pathetic clump just a few steps from the house as the flames died down.

After a few seconds, the front wall burst open. A body flew through the air, bounced a few times then slid several feet, spinning slightly, until coming to a stop. It didn't move, and neither did we.

The front of the house bulged and finally exploded outward, sending shards of wood and debris out toward us. Another monster stepped out of the hole. It looked like a giant ball of snot come to life. Parts faded in and out of view as though it wasn't really there. It held what appeared to be a thigh bone so dark it could've been crafted from ebony. The thigh bone glowed and pulsed purple-black. Circling the monster were some kind of ghosts or spirits. They were whitish and translucent, with ragged holes for mouths and eyes. The ghosts were screaming and moaning.

"Oh shit," said Brother Malachi, but the sound was distant, as though he were speaking underwater.

There was a buzzing in my ear that I tried to ignore as I peered harder at the creature and it slowly moved forward. Some part of my brain gibbered, but there was something so fascinating, so compelling about it, I couldn't look away. The creature's rippling gait, the flashing as parts of it shimmered in and out of existence, and the circling movement of the ghosts—there was something there, some secret I needed to know. Some new fantastic truth I needed to learn. I was still staring at it when I was tackled.

The impact broke the trance. My stomach rebelled, and acidic chunks of half-digested food filled my mouth, dribbling out and onto the ground. I was roughly jerked up and dragged away, face down. After a minute, I was able to get my feet under me, and I was half walking, half stumbling, still needing to be supported and shaky. Sounds become sharper, and I could hear Brother Malachi screaming over the radio.

"Night Stalker. I say again, Night Stalker. Fall back. Full release."

The gunfire started off slowly, but quickly grew in volume. Machine guns barked madly, and a hollow *thump thump thumping* like a mortar being fired added to the noise. Explosions cracked out, and an elephantine roar rent the air. We kept moving, Brother Malachi steadying me so I stayed upright and continuing to yell over the radio.

"Where are the snipers? We need every gun on that before it fully manifests."

A huge burst of purple-black further darkened the night sky. There were the sounds of crashing and, faintly, a scream. We made it back to the vehicles, got behind one, and Brother Malachi just dropped me. I collapsed to my knees, my strength returning and my head clear, but when I started to get back up, Brother Malachi put a boot to my chest and pushed me over. Keeping one foot on my chest, he reached into his combat vest. He pulled out his rosary and dropped it on my face. I was scared for a second, but the beads and metal felt cool, leeching the heat out of me.

"Thank God," he said and took his foot off my chest. "Get up, and don't look at it directly."

It took me a second as I was still a bit wobbly, but I did as commanded. I held out the rosary to him as I looked at what was happening.

The creature had moved off what was left of the porch and into the yard, still trying to advance despite the hail of bullets striking it. It seemed diminished, smaller. It waved the bone and another flash of purple-black shot out, colliding with an SUV. Flames washed over the vehicle, and it began to melt. The gas tank exploded with a pushing thwump of air, and a ball of flame rose up, illuminating the area.

The ghosts were gone, and the Night Stalker's body rippled from impacts. Little flares of silver hitting tainted flesh, instead of burning bright, were snuffed out. Larger rounds seemed to blow off layers of skin. I looked past it at the house, which was now sagging toward us and burning, but without the popping and snapping of a normal fire. While there was illumination, there was no heat from the flames.

Thump thump thump went something, and I turned, trying to see what was making the sound, but SUVs were in the way.

"What was that?" I asked Brother Malachi.

"Grenade launcher. Very unsubtle, and only used in emergencies."

The bark of sniper rifles sounded, and I turned back toward the house, not looking directly at the creature. It had shrunk even more, down to maybe half its original size. Once again shimmering, large pieces disappearing, it started to wave the bone again then blinked out of existence, imploding with a scream of hate and fury. Wind rushed past us, and there was a moment of utter stillness. Then the groans and screams began.

CHAPTER 38

We lost nine Hammers.

Brother Greg must've looked at the creature for too long. Another monk found him staring at nothing, drooling, his mind gone. Brother Ted, a behemoth of a man that others swore had a beautiful singing voice, was one of those killed by the ward. Brother Sammy, the shortest student in our class, was too close to the exploding SUV and was crushed. I stopped looking at the faces and bodies as it was too depressing.

You lived.

I was both elated and stricken by the thought. My stomach curled up on itself, and I had to keep a smile off my face. We weren't done, and I got to work. Brother Malachi and I helped with the cleanup and body retrieval as more vehicles arrived. The Master Hammer's face appeared to have new worry lines etched into it. He was dirty and even more beaten down. I didn't want to be him, or like him, carrying all that pain and knowledge around everywhere I went.

"Sebastian, come here," called Brother Malachi.

I walked over. He was standing next to the body that had been thrown through the front of the house. It was already steaming and bubbling.

"Is that him?" he asked.

Time stopped as I stared down at what was left of Thaddeus. The face was warped and twisted, but I knew it was him. There was no emotion as I gazed down, no desire to kick the corpse as a final "fuck you." I'd wanted so badly to eradicate this warlock. To avenge my wife. To get revenge for messing with my mind. Now that he was gone, I felt nothing. No happiness, no sense of completion, or satisfaction.

Looking back up at Brother Malachi, I said, "Yeah, it's Thaddeus."

"Nothing, huh?" he asked, peering at me, his brows furrowed in concentration.

"No. I expected something, but I don't feel anything."

"Good." He walked away.

I looked back down one last time and walked over to Brother Malachi. He was staring off toward the desert.

"So now what?" I asked.

He glanced at me. "Still want to learn? Want to be my apprentice?"

I thought for a second. It wasn't like I could ever go back. I was still wanted for the murder of my wife. Still banished from New England for making the bishop look bad. I didn't really want to be a Hammer, and I still had so many questions.

"Yes," I said, "if you'll have me."

"Of course."

"So what's next?"

"We go after whoever summoned that Night Stalker."

"Good plan."

The Master Hammer walked over to us, and stopped a few feet short. "Brother Sebastian, a moment of your time please."

I stepped over to him. "How may I help?" I asked formally.

"First, I want you to know that your final was not a setup."

I started to raise a hand tell him I was past that, but he stopped me by going on.

"No. It's important you know. It was an oversight on our part, an accident, not something malicious."

I nodded, and he continued.

"Despite being given an impossible mission, you did it. You Purged a warlock solo. Not many could do that. Well done."

"It wasn't the first time, Master Hammer."

"I know." He held up his hand, showing me his Hammer ring. The gold crosses gleamed weakly in the light. "You earned one of these before even becoming a

198

Hammer. I got mine because everyone else died. You," he shook his head and said softly, "you were all alone. Then you came here, under a bit of a cloud, and you excelled. You never repeated a class, mentored several others, helped them graduate as well. Then there's all of this," he said, sweeping an arm out at the burning building and monks cleaning up. "I'm told you took out a construct. Is that correct?"

"It was myself and Brother Malachi," I said quietly.

"Impressive." He paused for a second, staring at me. "We need you. You've done well, and I'd like you to lead a team, and maybe help Proctor the next class."

I felt the blush of pride at being asked, but did my best to keep from smiling. It would've been wrong in the middle of all this death and destruction. Still, I was pleased. I had earned their acceptance and trust. At one time, such an offer would've meant the world to me, I would've jumped at the chance, but now…now it didn't fit. I admired the Hammers, but didn't want to be one of them. I looked down for a long minute, trying to find the words.

"I'm honored, Master Hammer," I said as I looked up at him, "but I've agreed to be Brother Malachi's apprentice for the time being."

He sucked in a breath over his teeth, surprise showing on his face. He blinked at me a few times then glanced over at Brother Malachi and said, "I understand. You've chosen a hard road to follow. A righteous one, a necessary one, but it's a dark path. God shine his light on you. You will always be welcome here." He turned on his heel and walked stiffly back to the others.

I went back to Brother Malachi, who must've heard what was said. "Offer you a job?"

"Yes. Team leader or Proctor."

"You'd do well here."

I shook my head. "They're too…constrained, too set in their ways, like a French knight charging through a muddy field toward the English archers. Rigid thinking. I wouldn't fit or last. I want more."

He nodded and leaned in toward me. "Maybe you're right. Let's help finish this clean up." He waggled his eyebrows at me. "Then, we have a mystery to solve." With that, he turned and walked off.

"That's so wrong," I said, once I closed my mouth, and he chuckled as I followed.

EPILOGUE

Top flew erratically, with dips and swerves, barely able to go forward. The silver burned so much, and the gnawing on his mind as the other pushed and tried to assert dominance made it difficult to concentrate. Finally, the pain and distractions were too much, and he landed. Poorly. Another spasm rocked his body, and the change began. The convulsions were getting stronger and the mind pushing on his grew more insistent. He wouldn't be able to hold out much longer. Soon, he'd be no more. The pain curled him into a ball. Between the contractions, he heard footsteps approach.

Top opened his eyes and saw a shadow, a dark spot blotting out the night sky.

"Hello, Thaddeus. Too bad you failed, but at least I have a new servant now."

The voice was *wrong*, but spoke clarity and compulsion. Unable to withstand the pain, Top blacked out.

About the Author

A storyteller who's woven the real with the fantastic since he was a child, Lincoln is an Army Reservist who's had the pleasure of visiting the Middle East five times so far. He currently resides in the Commonwealth of Virginia with his lovely wife, little girl, and Calvin the Helper Dog. When not doing obscure jobs for the Government or shadowy corporations, he works at honing his craft and defeating the neighborhood ninjas.

Connect with me online:

Twitter: @LincolnFarish
Blog: http://farishsfreehold.blogspot.com/
Facebook: https://www.facebook.com/lincoln.farish.7

33479775R00114

Made in the USA
Middletown, DE
15 July 2016